Fractured Lives

TARA CONRAD

HIS ONE HER ONLY PUBLISHING

Contents

Svetlana

"Yes, Papa. Pyotr checked out the dorm. He was happy with the security," I explain for the tenth time. My cell is propped on the small counter so I can keep the call on speaker while I finish putting away the groceries I picked up.

"Does he have a key for your room? In case there is an emergency."

I love Papa with all my heart, but he tends to go overboard. "Yes, he has the key card." I roll my eyes.

"Would you consider him staying in the dorm for one semester? I will make the arrangements."

Putting some distance between myself and everything that comes with being a Solonik is one of the biggest reasons I wanted to come to New York City. I thought going to Moscow would be far enough, but it wasn't. Papa's reputation runs far and wide, especially in Russia. I hoped by coming here, I'd have a fresh start as just Svetlana Solonik. If Pyotr lives in the dorms like he has in the past, it's going to raise red flags with my classmates, and they'll avoid me like they did in Moscow.

"Papa, we talked about this. I don't want Pyotr living in the dorm with me."

"I know, *moya babochka,*" he sighs in defeat. "I had to try."

The door to my dorm opens, startling me. An older man and woman walk in, followed by a petite girl with long blonde curls. "Papa, I have to go. My roommate just arrived." I end the call and, slide my phone into my pocket, and am ready to introduce myself.

"I thought you had a single room." The woman whispers loudly.

"They're first come, first serve. I guess they ran out." The girl turns to me and smiles. "Hi. I'm Natalie."

"I'm Svetlana. It's nice to meet you."

"These are my parents, Charlo—"

"Mr. and Mrs. Clarke," the woman interrupts.

"It's a pleasure to meet you both. Is there anything I can do to help?"

Natalie goes to speak, but Mrs. Clarke steps in front and answers for her daughter. "We've got it just fine on our own."

Sensing the hostility from her mother, I decide it's best to give them some privacy. "Okay. I'll get out of your way."

The dorms at NYU are much different than in Moscow, where Mei and I shared a single space that was both our sleeping and study area. Here, the rooms are set up like small apartments with two private bedrooms that share a kitchen and bathroom.

I go into my room and close the door. Unfortunately, the walls in our rooms are paper-thin, and I can hear everything.

"I'm going to find whoever's in charge here and speak to them. You need a room by yourself."

"I'm fine. I think it'll be fun to have a dormmate."

"Did you hear her accent? She sounds like she's from Russia or some foreign place like that."

What's this woman's problem? My impulsive side wants to text Pyotr and ask him to come over. That would definitely give her something to complain about, but I don't want to ruin any chance of becoming friends with my roommate.

"Charlotte, I think it'll be good for Natalie to share the space." Mr. Clarke makes his opinion known.

Just like she did with her daughter, Mrs. Clarke overrules her husband. "You're far too permissive, Stanley."

"I'll be fine, I promise. If you guys don't get going, you'll miss your flight."

"Are you sure you want to stay?" Their voices grow louder. They must be in the kitchen. "It's not too late to come home. You'll be much closer to Thomas."

"I'm positive."

After what sounds like a tearful goodbye on the mother's part, they finally leave. A few seconds later, there's a soft knock on my door.

"I apologize for my parents' behavior," Natalie says when I open the door. "They aren't thrilled that I'm going to school here. They're even less happy that I have a roommate."

"My parents weren't exactly over the moon with me choosing NYU either. But why wouldn't they want you to have a roommate?"

"They, well, mostly my mother, are afraid I'll be negatively influenced by people who don't live the way we do." She shrugs. "Other than the times they've dropped me off here, they rarely leave the smalltown I live in."

"Parents," I chuckle. "There's nothing to apologize for. Where are you from?"

"Northmeadow. It's a small town in Missouri." I must look as clueless as I feel because I'm not sure where that is in relation to New York. "It's in the Midwestern part of the country," she explains. "Where are you from?"

"St. Petersburg, Russia."

"Wow. What brought you here?"

"I was looking to experience something different."

"New York certainly fits the bill for that."

"It certainly does."

"Would you like to grab a bite to eat?" she asks.

"I'd love to. Do you know any place good?"

"I know a little Russian restaurant a few blocks away."

Svetlana

The restaurant is only three blocks from our dorm. Although the food isn't exactly the Russian fare I'm used to eating, it's not bad, and having food that's somewhat familiar is comforting.

"You said you were from a small town. How small is small?"

"There's less than one thousand people."

"Excuse me?" I nearly choke on my bite of food. "Did you say one thousand?"

"Yep. It's the kind of place where everyone knows everyone."

"I kind of understand that. St. Petersburg has over five million citizens, but our direct community is small."

"It can be suffocating," she says.

We finish our meal and start our walk back to campus just as the sun's beginning to set. As much as I fought Papa to let me be more independent, being out alone is an unfamiliar feeling, and I find myself looking around to find Pyotr. I texted him before I left the dorm, so I know he's following us. But just as Papa promised, Pyotr's staying out of sight.

"Is everything okay?" Natalie asks.

"Yes. Why?"

"You look nervous."

"A little. St. Petersburg may have a lot of people, but it's nothing like this. I guess it's going to take a little getting used to." I don't want to talk much about myself, so I attempt to change the subject. "What brought you here?"

"My brother."

"Does he live here too?"

"I wish. But, no. Michael committed suicide two years ago."

"I'm so sorry."

"Thank you," Natalie says sadly. "His death changed my whole perspective on life."

"Loss has a way of doing that."

"Before he died, my only plan was to marry my boyfriend and become a mother. I still want to do those things," she says quickly. "But I also want to get my degree and have a job."

"What are you studying?"

"Psychology. I plan to become a therapist."

"That's terrific. I'm sure your parents are very proud of you."

"Not exactly."

"Why not?"

"My parents expected me to get married right after high school like they did. They weren't thrilled when I told them I wanted to attend college. Then, I told them I wanted to attend NYU. Mom was completely against it. If it wasn't for my scholarship, I wouldn't be here." Natalie's phone dings. When she checks the screen, a huge grin spreads across her face. "It's my boyfriend, Tommy." She holds it up, and I see a picture of a handsome guy with dirty blonde hair and a mega-watt smile. He's wearing a sports jersey and holding an American football.

"He's gorgeous."

"He is," Natalie says dreamily. "Give me a second." She types a quick text and sends it off.

"How long have you two been dating?"

"Since we were fifteen."

During our meal, Natalie told me a little about North-meadow, the ultra-conservative small town she grew up in. Now, all this about getting married and popping out babies immediately after secondary education. That's a crazy old-fashioned idea —even for Eastern Europe.

"Wow. That's a long time. Does he go to NYU, too?"

"No. Tommy would never leave Missouri. He got a full-ride football scholarship at Mizzou.

"What's a *Mizzou*?" I struggle with the word.

"It's the nickname for the University of Missouri."

"It must be hard being so far apart."

"It's been challenging, but we're making it work."

It wasn't easy only seeing Slava on weekends, and we weren't even really dating. One of the reasons I didn't sign another contract with him was because of the extreme distance my going to school in the United States would put between us. I give her a lot of credit for being able to handle a long-distance relationship.

"Do you have a boyfriend?" she asks.

"I was seeing someone back in Russia, but we broke up shortly before I came here. It's all good, though. New York is a big city with lots of possibilities."

"I guess," she says.

"What do you like to do on weekends?" I ask as we arrive back at our dorm, hoping to get the scoop on places to hang out.

"Except for a few local restaurants, I don't go off campus."

I stop dead in my tracks. "You mean to tell me you've been in this city for over a year, and you haven't gone to any clubs or bars?"

"Tommy doesn't approve of me going to places like that." She shrugs, and before I can respond, her phone rings again. "It's Tommy. I better take this. Hello?" Natalie answers her phone as she walks into her bedroom, closing the door behind her.

Her boyfriend doesn't *approve* of her going out? Something tells me he's not sitting in his dorm every weekend worrying about her. Why should Natalie have to miss out on everything college life has to offer? The more I dwell on this, the more I decide I don't like this Tommy guy.

Brandon

Much to Maxim and Pyotr's dismay, Alex and I moved Lana into her dorm a few weeks ago. They would've been happy if she had decided to stay with Alex rather than move onto campus. I understand her need for autonomy, especially given her father's high profile.

"You looked stressed," Alex says from my office doorway.

"It's nice to see you, too," I say as he walks in.

"What's going on?"

"Svetlana."

Alex sinks into one of the chairs. "What did she do now?"

"She didn't do anything." I close my laptop and sigh. "I'm nervous about seeing her tonight."

Alex is bringing Svetlana to Fire and Ice. I'm looking forward to it since I haven't seen her in several weeks. We've kept in touch by text and phone and have gotten to know one another better. Svetlana's an intelligent young woman with a mind of her own, which I've found surprisingly attractive. Nothing compares to spending time in person, though. My mind has been wandering all day, which makes working next to impossible.

"That's all?" Alex chuckles.

"She keeps herself pretty closed off. I don't exactly know what she's hoping for between us."

"Svetlana's a difficult one to figure out. Just when you think you understand her, she sheds a layer, and you have to start over again," Alex chuckles but shifts his mood back to seriousness when he notices I'm not laughing with him. "Something tells me that's not what you're worried about."

"I don't want to repeat past mistakes."

"What happened between you and Celia was a long time ago," Alex tries reassuring me.

"The past has a habit of creeping up on us when we least expect it."

"That night was awful. I'm not trying to downplay what happened. But it wasn't your fault. You were young and didn't know anything about the lifestyle."

"That's not an excuse."

"I'm not trying to make excuses. You took the advice of people you were supposed to be able to trust. You were as much a victim as Celia."

"Don't ever say that. Celia was the only victim that night."

"Brand," Alex says, lowering his voice. "You suffered as much as she did."

"I shouldn't have had that drink. If I didn't make that choice, things would be—."

"If I thought for a second that you weren't trustworthy, I wouldn't have agreed to let you pursue Svetlana," Alex interrupts. "How she'll react when you offer her a contract is anyone's guess."

"She's really not like everyone makes her out."

"Lana's a challenge, and she's often unpredictable," Alex says thoughtfully. "But you're right. Underneath her protective exterior is a kind and caring young woman."

"It sounds like your perspective on her has changed."

"Living with her all summer, I've seen a different side of her. There's still plenty of days I'd like to wring her neck, though," Alex chuckles.

While Svetlana was staying with Alex, I was able to spend a good amount of time with her. Alex is right. She does a remarkable job of maintaining a prickly disguise, ensuring most people don't stick around for long. For those that aren't chased away, they earn the opportunity to see the real Svetlana. The one who's fun-loving and flirty but who's also incredibly vulnerable.

"She's complex," I admit.

"And I think you're the right man to help her let her guard down once and for all."

"I don't know about that."

"Enough of the self-deprecating talk." Alex waves me off. "Are you going to propose negotiating a contract tonight?"

"I have a private room reserved," I say, leaning back in my chair.

"That sounds like it could be fun."

"Don't get excited. It's only so we'll have a quiet place to talk." Alex raises his eyebrows, clearly not believing me.

As much as I miss seeing Lana whenever I'm at Alex's, her being busy with the start of a new semester hasn't been entirely negative. We've discussed the lifestyle and what we both want for our future. I know she wants a permanent Dominant, and she knows I'm interested in her as a submissive.

Tonight, I plan to ask my little *papillion* to begin vetting and negotiating a contract.

Brandon

ALEX IS RUNNING LATE, WHICH MEANS LANA IS ALSO running late. I alternate between leaning against the building and pacing back and forth on the sidewalk in front of Fire and Ice, waiting for them to arrive. My nerves are on a hairpin trigger, thinking about the many ways tonight could turn out.

Finally, I see Alex's car coming down the street. Viktor slows to a stop, and I step forward to open the backdoor and help Lana out. Once she's on her feet, I allow my gaze to travel up and down her body. She's wearing tight jeans that accentuate her long, lean legs and a black top that's low cut and held together by several thin straps.

"You look amazing."

"Thank you," she answers.

"Montgomery," I greet my friend as he exits the car. He holds up a finger, and I see he's on his phone.

"He's had that thing glued to him all afternoon," Lana complains.

"It must be important."

"It's Papa. There's information he needs pushed through the network."

"One minute, Max," Alex says, moving the phone away from

his ear. "You two go ahead without me. I have to go back to the office."

"Do you need a hand? I can go with you."

"I'd prefer if you stay and keep an eye on Lana."

She crosses her arms. "I don't need a babysitter."

That's when I realize whatever's going on with Max must be important because Alex doesn't engage. Instead, he puts the phone back to his ear and slides into his car.

"Shall we?" I hold the club door open for Lana and follow her inside.

Like most other weekend nights, Fire and Ice is busy. The three stages have scenes in progress, and the private rooms are either in use or reserved. I'm glad I called ahead. "I reserved one of the suites. Are you comfortable with that?"

"Of course." She smiles.

We make our way through the main area where the majority of the action is taking place. The hallway is empty as we walk down to room three. I swipe my member id under the scanner on the door, and the lock clicks open.

Lana steps in and looks around. I reserved a role-play room that's set up like a classroom with a blackboard, a teacher's desk, and several student desks arranged in neat rows. Several of the desks have built-in restraints, and there's a variety of paddles and rulers to discipline any deserving pupils.

Lana leans against one of the desks. "Are you into a teacher/student kink?"

"Not particularly. This room is the most conducive room for talking."

"Talking, right," Lana says, sitting at a desk. "Where should we start, Mr. Carpenter?"

"You can call me Brandon." I grab the chair behind the teacher's desk and drag it around to sit across from Lana. "How's school so far?"

"It's been quite an adjustment. University here is much different than in Russia."

"How so?"

"In Russia, we choose our major, but our classes and schedule are chosen for us. No changes can be made to the schedule. Classes start at eight a.m. every morning and don't end until well into the afternoon."

"That sounds pretty strict."

"It is. But here, I was able to choose my classes and schedule. It's a very different experience, but so far, I like it."

"I'm glad to hear that." My statement is followed by an awkward silence. I'm not sure what to ask or say next. When we're texting or on the phone, we never run out of things to talk about. But sitting here alone together is a different story. I don't know what to say next.

Lana's the first one to break the silence. "What are we doing here?"

"What do you mean?"

"This." She motions around us. "We haven't seen each other in weeks. You went through the trouble of reserving a private room. And you only want to talk."

"Yes." The word comes out sounding just as uncertain as I'm feeling.

"Look, Brandon, I'm really interested in you."

"I'm interested in you, too."

"Why am I getting the feeling there's something you aren't saying?"

"There is."

"Tell me."

None of this is going like I planned. "I'm not ready to discuss a Dom/sub contract. I want to keep seeing you, but I understand if you aren't interested." The words come out fast, and they were not the ones I intended to say. What the hell was that, Brandon? I mentally chastise myself.

"That's all?" Lana gets up and walks around the desk until she's standing before me. "I'm okay with that, for now." She runs her finger down my chest. "So, do we have this room all night?"

"We do."

"How about we put it to good use?"

Even though I know I shouldn't do this, I can't help myself. My hands grip her waist, pulling her onto my lap. "Before we go any further, I need to know this is okay with you. That this is what you want."

"It is."

"What is? I want to know exactly what you want." I allow myself to slip back into the Dominant role I'm most comfortable in.

"I want you to fuck me, Mr. Carpenter."

Those words are exactly what I needed to hear. My lips crash against hers, and she opens, granting my tongue access as I deepen the kiss. She pulls away and slides off my lap. Her hands slide her shirt up and over her head. It lands on the floor. Then she moves to her jeans, unbuttoning them and shimmying them down her legs. She kicks them aside. Lana stands before me in nothing but a black lace bra and a scrap of fabric that covers her pussy.

"How can I please you?" she asks seductively.

"Turn around and bend over the desk," I say in a low, deep voice.

Lana's graceful as she turns her back to me and folds herself over the desk.

I grab the ruler off the teacher's desk and bring it over to show her. "Is it okay to use this on you?"

"I would love that, Mr. Carpenter.

"If it's too much, all you need to do is tell me to stop. Do you understand?"

"Yes, I understand."

Lana's already told me she loves impact play and that she craves pain, so I feel comfortable with the way this is going.

The wooden ruler makes contact with Lana's ass. I know it stings, but she doesn't flinch. I do the same on the other side. Her pale skin turns pink. "How's that?"

"Not hard enough."

My strikes don't have to be hard to make a significant impact. Instead, I hit her five times quickly, all in the same area. A soft mewl escapes her lips.

I pause to pull my shirt over my head and toss it to the teacher's desk. "Your ass is a beautiful shade of red, *mon petit papillon.* How does it feel?"

"It feels good. May I have more?"

"You're a greedy little thing, aren't you?"

"Yes," she says.

Without warning, the ruler makes contact with her skin. "Do you act this way with other professors?"

"No, Mr. Carpenter. Only you," she says in a breathy tone.

"Good. If I'm fucking you, no one else better come near you." Dropping the ruler, I take her black panties and pull. They tear easily, and I let them fall to the floor. Then, I reach my hand between her legs. "This pussy is all mine."

"Mhm."

"Say it, Svetlana. Tell me it's mine."

"My pussy is yours." I slide my finger inside her. "I'm wet for you."

"You're dripping." I add another finger, pumping them in and out. "Spread your legs."

I open my pants and free my dick. I line it up with her opening and push inside as far as her body can take me. Then, I pull out. Lana whimpers and my hand smacks her ass before I slide back inside.

"Hold onto the desk, and don't let go." Her hands reach over the top of the desk and grasp it tightly. As soon as they do, I pull almost all the way out before I thrust into her hard and fast. With my hands holding onto her hips, I repeat the punishing move over and over.

I know I should slow down and ease up my hold on her. She's going to have bruises from my fingers, but I don't care. I want to mark her—make her mine.

"Come for me, Svetlana," I demand. "Fucking tell me your mine while you come on my cock."

"I'm yours," she yells as her body squeezes mine, sending me into my own orgasm. "Oh my God, you feel so good, Mr. Carpenter."

When I pull out, I watch my cum drip from her pussy. It's an erotic sight that I can't take my eyes off.

"Did I pass your test?" she asks, looking over her shoulder.

"I think I can give you an A for today." I take her by the hand and help her up. "Are you okay? I didn't hurt you, did I?"

"You don't have to worry about hurting me," she says. "Contract or not, I like it rough."

I don't know how or why I was lucky enough to meet this woman. But now that I've had her, I'll be damned if I let anyone or anything take her away.

Svetlana

AFTER STRAIGHTENING MYSELF UP IN THE ATTACHED bathroom, I return to the classroom where Brandon's finishing cleaning up.

"It seems we've missed tonight's scenes," he says.

"I guess it's good I didn't come to see them."

"True. It wasn't *them* you came for," Brandon grins.

"Was that a joke?" Brandon's always so serious. I like seeing this side of him, too.

"Alex texted. He's still tied up at the office. If you'd like, I can drive you back to your dorm."

"I'm planning on staying at Alex's tonight. Natalie doesn't know about all this, and I'd like to keep it that way."

Our lives are polar opposites. It's not only our geography but how we were raised. My parents live the BDSM lifestyle and have always been open and willing to talk about anything. Well, almost anything. Stanley and Charlotte Clarke are ultra-religious and conservative. Natalie was raised with such closed-minded views. It's a wonder she's as open as she is. Natalie's sweet and innocent —I adore that about her. But she's also very naïve. I'm afraid if I told her about this part of me, she'd run in the opposite direction and never look back.

"That's fine. I can take you there," Brandon says, taking my hand in his as we walk across the club's main room. "I don't have a fancy driver like your father or Alex."

I stop walking. "I don't care about any of that stuff." Brandon cocks his head. "I know you've been told I'm a spoiled princess, and in some ways, I guess it's true. Papa's job ensured I was raised with advantages not everyone had. But I don't care about money or status. Actually, I think I'd be happier with nothing."

Brandon takes a few steps, closing the distance between us. "I don't give a shit what anyone else thinks. I know what I see when I look at you, *mon petit papillon*, and that's all that matters."

"What's *papillon?*"

"It's French for butterfly. You," Brandon cups my cheek in his hand. "Are a beautiful and mysterious butterfly."

"Why did you call me that?"

"Butterflies symbolize hope, bravery, and transformation. Everything you embody." Goosebumps cover my arms, and I shiver. "Are you okay?"

"I'm good." This is getting too personal, and I try to pull away.

"No, you aren't." His hold on me tightens. "Why did that bother you?"

I want to run, but for some reason, my mouth betrays me and opens, allowing words to spill out. "Papa and Pyotr have called me butterfly since I was a little girl. There's no way you could've known that, yet you called me butterfly, too."

"Then, you know it's true," Brandon says. I lean in to kiss him and am interrupted by my phone rings. "You should answer that."

I nod and take a step back, then reach into my pocket to pull out my phone. "Hello?"

"Hey. I'm sorry I got tied up here," Alex says. "I wanted to check in on you."

"There's nothing to be sorry for. Is everything okay there?"

"Your father had some critical information that needed to get into the right hands. Thankfully, it did."

"I'm glad to hear that."

"Brandon texted to let me know he's driving you home."

"Is it okay if I stay at your apartment tonight?"

"Of course."

"Thanks." I smile.

"I'm wrapping everything up here, so I shouldn't be much longer. I'll see you in a bit."

After I hang up, I join Brandon, who's talking with Star. "Is everything okay?"

"It is." I'm not sure what, if anything, Star knows about Alex and Brandon's involvement in Papa's business, so I don't say anything else.

"I'm going to have you wait with Star while I get the car." Brandon kisses my cheek before turning to walk away.

I watch him until he's out of sight.

Most everyone has cleared out of the club. With the lights low and the music off, it's quiet in here—too quiet. Star's finishing some paperwork, but she keeps stopping and looking at me. I scroll down my social media, trying to appear busy. I hope she thinks I'm too busy to talk, but of course, that doesn't work.

"How was your evening?" Star asks.

"It was nice." I glance up quickly and then go back to scrolling.

"I didn't see you and Brandon for most of the night."

"We were around."

"Mhm." She taps her papers on the table. "By around, I suppose you mean in a private room all night."

"Yes." I put the phone down. "We had some important matters to discuss."

"I know Brandon and am certain of your safety with him. Otherwise, this conversation would be very different. I'd be remiss if I didn't remind you of the need to vet a Dominant before being intimate with them."

"Yes, I'm aware. That would only be if the relationship were of a contractual nature, correct?" My reply comes out snippier than I intended, but at the same time, I get tired of always being treated like a child.

"That's correct."

Brandon: I'm out front in the red Mustang.

"Brandon's here. Have a good night." I quickly head for the door.

"Svetlana," Star calls.

"Yes?" I stop and turn around.

"I'm not the enemy here. If you're open to it, we might even get to be friends."

It isn't what I expected her to say, and I find myself momentarily at a loss for words. I recover slightly and mumble, "Goodnight."

Brandon

"WHAT THE HELL WERE YOU THINKING?" ALEX YELLS, and I hold the phone away from my ear.

"Hello to you, too." I roll my eyes.

"Whatever. Answer my question."

"Why?"

"Because that's my collar around her neck."

"Collar of protection," I say, irritated. "She's not your submissive."

"Svetlana's my responsibility to protect."

"Weren't you giving me the lecture earlier on how much you trust me?"

"Yes, but that didn't mean you should go and fuck her tonight."

"Wait a damn minute. How do you know what we did or didn't do?"

"After Lana didn't respond to my texts, I called Star. She informed me you and Svetlana were in the private room all night. That can only mean one thing."

"We're both consenting adults."

"Who should be vetting one another, not—"

"There's no contract, so there's no need for vetting."

"Right."

"I'm serious."

"What happened?"

"I told Lana I'm not ready for a contract, and by some stroke of luck, she was okay with it. What happened after that is between Lana and me."

"You're serious? You're not pursuing her as a submissive?" Alex asks, lowering his voice.

"Don't mistake this for being disinterested. I'm still very much pursuing her. We're just not looking at a dynamic right now."

"Oh." There's an awkward pause. "I apologize for jumping to conclusions."

"It's all good. But Montgomery, you're way too uptight. You need to get yourself laid." I laugh.

"Fuck off, Carpenter."

"I'm hanging up now. I need to get back to the club."

"Where the hell are you?"

"I'm walking down west twenty-third."

"Where's Lana?"

"I left her on a street corner," I say sarcastically.

"What the hell?" Alex yells.

"Lana's with Star at the club. I went to get the car."

"You're lucky. Now get off the damn phone and get back to Lana."

I can't contain my laughter, earning me side-eyed looks from people who try to avoid walking by me on the sidewalk.

The garage I use when I'm at the club is only a few blocks away, but I didn't want Lana to have to walk. I get the car and return to the club in less than fifteen minutes. There's no parking, so I put my flashers on and text Lana, letting her know I'm here. She comes out almost immediately.

"Nice ride," she says appreciatively.

"You like Valkyrie?" I run my hand along the dash.

"I did until I knew it was a she." Lana pouts.

"I didn't take you for the jealous type."

"You're running your hands over another woman. What do you expect?"

"Valkyrie is beautiful, but she has nothing on you."

"Smooth," Lana chuckles.

I reach over her and grab the safety belt, clicking it into place. "Being properly restrained is important."

"I'm a huge supporter of restraints." I love that she keeps up the witty banter.

The radio plays in the background while I drive up Riverside Blvd. "Tell me something about you I don't know yet."

Lana responds quickly, "I don't have a driver's license."

"Really?" I don't know why that surprises me. It's fairly normal for people who've grown up in Manhattan to not have a license. Public transportation can take you everywhere you need to go. Anyone who's ever driven downtown will attest to what a nightmare it is. I only got mine to drive my parents back and forth to their many doctor's appointments.

"Since I've always had a guard to bring me wherever I need to go, there's never been a reason for me to have one."

"Do you want to learn to drive?"

"I never really thought about it." She shrugs. "Living in the city, I don't see a reason to have one since I can walk or take the subway anywhere I need to go." Lana shifts in her seat to face me. "Tell me something about you."

"What do you want to know?"

"Do you have any siblings?"

"I have an older sister."

"Are you close?"

"No. By the time I was born, she was grown and out of the house."

"Does your sister live in the city?"

"She's in Germany with her husband. We don't really keep in touch."

"I'd give anything to have my sister back," Lana says pensively. "You should try to talk to yours more."

I glance over at Lana. The faraway look on her face makes me realize how callous my words must've sounded. I know how much Lana misses her sister, and I've taken for granted that I still have mine. "You're right. I should."

I enter the parking garage under Alex's building and pull into the guest parking spot.

"I had a nice time tonight," Lana says.

"Tonight's not over."

"It isn't?" Her face lights up.

"I'll wait with you until Alex gets home."

Svetlana

Brandon and I are enjoying a glass of red wine when Alex strolls into the kitchen.

"Hello, you two," he says as he loosens his tie.

"You look like shit," Brandon says.

I look at Brandon and raise my eyebrow before turning to Alex. "Would you like a glass of wine?"

"That'd be great," Alex says, ignoring Brandon's smart-ass comment.

While I get a glass, the guys talk quietly. "What was going on that had you tied up all night."

"A large shipment was on the move from Cyprus to Venezuela. I needed to push the information through to Max's contacts in South America and wait for their reply."

"Were they successful in intercepting?"

"The raid was wrapping up when I left," Alex says as I hand him the glass. "Tomorrow, we'll start placing the recovered persons in treatment facilities."

Papa works tirelessly, trying to stop human trafficking. One of the biggest hurdles is trafficking is a multi-billion-dollar business. Where there's that kind of money, there's sure to be a fight. Over the years, Papa's network has grown, expanding all over the globe. Unfortunately, the traffickers have shared the same growth. That doesn't stop Papa and all the others from continuing the fight with the hope that one day, we'll live in a world free from this evil crime.

"Where will they go?" I ask. "Jelena's Hope is almost at capacity."

"There are a few smaller facilities," Alex explains. "We'll do our best to ensure no one is left without the services they need."

I swirl the wine around my glass.

"What are you thinking?" Brandon asks.

"After we found out Jelena had been murdered." The sting of those words is still as piercing as the day it happened. My thoughts come out disjointed. "Sometimes I wonder what I'm doing here. Going to school seems like a waste of time when I could be back home working at the center and making a real difference."

"Just because you aren't there doesn't mean you're not making a difference. You're studying to become a lawyer to help put the criminals involved in trafficking behind bars." Brandon reminds me.

"I guess."

It's not that he's wrong. In my mind, that was my plan from the beginning. Looking back, I can't help but think how naïve I was. Why did I think I could go head-to-head with traffickers in a court of law? First off, how many of them actually get arrested? Out of those, even fewer end up in front of a judge. And if by some chance they do, realistically, what are my chances of winning a trial? They pay their legal counsel a fortune to keep them out of prison. Corruption runs deep in these circles, and I'm no match for them.

"I don't want to hear, *I guess.*" Brandon places his hand over mine. "You've already made a huge difference in so many people's lives through Jelena's Hope. You'll continue to do so through the legal system. Will it be easy? Of course not. But if there's one thing I know about you, it's that you don't back down from a challenge."

"Sometimes it just seems like it's all for nothing. Papa works day and night, yet the trafficking industry hasn't really been affected. Who has he stopped?"

I don't know how Papa gets up every day and looks evil in the face, knowing that no matter how many traffickers he eliminates, there's more waiting in the shadows to step in and pick up where their predecessors left off.

"Svetlana," Alex interrupts my thoughts. "You're right that we'll never eradicate trafficking, but that doesn't mean our efforts are wasted. I'm certain every person who's walked through the doors of Jelena's Hope has a different opinion. None of this is for nothing."

I know Alex and Brandon are right, but that doesn't stop the doubt that creeps in, making me question everything.

Svetlana

"Thank you for tonight," I say as I walk Brandon to Alex's private elevator.

"I'd like to see you again."

"I'd like that, too."

Brandon leans in to kiss me goodnight. His erection presses against my abdomen, and I almost ask him to stay.

"When?" he asks as the elevator doors open.

"Maybe next weekend. I'll let you know if I'm going to be here."

"Can I see you before then?"

"I don't think so." I'm unsure how to navigate these waters. I'm looking for a Dominant, not a boyfriend. I know I told Brandon I'm okay with not pursuing a dynamic right now. I'm hoping I can convince him to not wait too long. "I'll text you during the week."

Brandon steps into the elevator. "Goodnight, Svetlana," he says as the doors close.

After he leaves, I return to the living room and sink onto the dark grey sofa. Alex follows me into the room and sits across from me. "How was your night?" he asks.

"It was nice."

"Nice?" He raises an eyebrow.

"Yes. Nice." I don't know how much Alex knows, and I'm certainly not going to be the one to kiss and tell.

"How were the scenes tonight?"

"Okay."

"I'm sorry I wasn't able to make it. I hope Brandon kept you entertained."

"I haven't seen him in a while, so it was nice to talk and catch up." It's a true statement.

"I see."

"Why the inquisition?" I ask, mildly annoyed.

"Look, I know what happened tonight." Alex leans forward, resting his elbows on his knees. "I need to be sure you know what you're doing."

"You're not my father, Alex."

"I'm well aware of that."

"Then, why are we having this conversation?"

"Because you're both my friends."

"And?"

"I don't want to see anyone get hurt."

"Thanks a lot," I snap and stand from the couch, intending to walk away.

"Lana—" Alex reaches out to grab my arm.

"Don't Lana me," I say as I spin around. "I know what everyone thinks about me. Do you think I don't hear what they say?"

"That's not what I'm doing. I'm trying to look out for you."

"I don't need you prying into my personal business." Alex runs his hand through his hair and lets out a frustrated sigh. This argument is pointless. Instead of continuing down this path, I decide to shift the direction of the conversation, hoping I can convince Alex to give me some information. "How long have you known Brandon?"

Sometimes, when we're together, I see a haunted look come over Brandon's face, but as quickly as it comes, it's gone. I assume whatever it is would explain why he's apprehensive about pursuing a Dom/sub dynamic. He's told me a little about himself, but I sense there's something important he's holding back.

"Nine years or so."

"How long has he been going to Fire and Ice?"

"Why do you ask?"

"When we talked tonight, I was sure he would ask me to start vetting. Instead, he said he wasn't interested in a dynamic, and I'm curious why not."

"What did he tell you?"

"Nothing."

"Then you won't get anything else from me either."

"What happened to wanting to protect me?" I cross my arms.

"That's exactly what I'm doing." Alex takes a step back. "When Brandon's ready, he'll tell you himself."

"So, you admit there's something."

"Goodnight, Svetlana. I'll see you in the morning."

I let out a frustrated groan. These men are infuriating.

Brandon (Two Years Later)

I'm startled awake from a nightmare. Sweat drips from my forehead, and I'm breathing heavily. Nightmares about that night with Celia have plagued my dreams for the past two years—since I started dating Svetlana.

Getting out of bed, I open the door to my small balcony and step outside. The clear sky allows the full moon to illuminate the night. A warm breeze blows and makes my sweat-drenched skin feel cool. I can't shake the memory of Celia's face when I finally realized what was happening.

Celia's eyes water and mascara drips down her face as I fuck her mouth while Diablo thrusts himself into her ass. The scene is erotic as hell, and I come in her throat. Celia swallows everything I give and then, with long, slow drags of her tongue, licks me clean.

I step away while Diablo continues to thrust into her. I won't leave Celia alone, but I need a drink. Cracking the door open, I spot Angel. "Would you grab me a beer?"

"Sure."

Behind me, Diablo's still balls deep inside Celia. "Do you like being a whore?" he asks.

"I do, Diablo." Celia loves to be shared, especially with Diablo.

He grabs her hips and comes with a roar. He pulls out and smacks her ass before going into the attached bathroom.

"Here you go." Angel looks over my shoulder into the room. "Fuck, Brandon. She's smoking hot. Do you have room for anyone else?"

With my glass in hand, I walk over to Celia. "Are you good with adding one more?"

"Yes, Master," she says and licks her bottom lip.

I motion for him to join us.

Angel walks into the room and straight over to Celia. I chug the rest of my beer, watching Angel whisper to her while he strokes her hair.

Diablo returns from the restroom and gives Angel a nod. "Are you almost ready, Brandon?" he asks.

"I'll be there in a minute." My words come out slurred. That's odd. I've only had one beer.

Angel steps away from Celia and grabs a ball gag from the wall. I try to ask him what he's doing, but when I go to open my mouth, nothing happens. My legs feel weak, and blackness creeps into the edge of my vision until there's nothing but blackness and silence.

A shiver runs through me. It's over, I remind myself. Except when I considered entering a serious dynamic, I became paralyzed. I know I'm not the same person I was back then, but fear is a cage holding me hostage. Its bars are made of my insecurities and doubts.

Shortly after I expressed interest in Svetlana, Alex removed his collar of protection. The plan was we'd vet and enter a dynamic. I've thought about it non-stop since then but haven't brought it up again. Since she's not in a dynamic, other Dominants have approached her asking to enter vetting with her. Hell, I don't blame them. Svetlana's a brilliant young woman who's also stunning. She told me she'd wait, and so far, she's turned them all down. But how much longer will that last? I'm afraid she'll get sick of waiting for me to man up. That Lana will take one of those men up on their offer and leave me in her past.

There's nothing that can be done right now. So, I force myself to take deep breaths to slow my heart rate. Once I'm sure I'm calm, I go back to bed and fall into a now dreamless sleep.

Svetlana

Undergrad school is finally in our rearview mirror. After my parents flew back to Russia, Natalie and I traveled to Northmeadow with her parents, where we've spent the past month. When I say she comes from a narrow-minded small town, I'm not exaggerating. I've never seen anything like it.

Charlotte treats Natalie like she's a child who's incapable of making any decisions on her own. If Natalie tries to assert herself, she's reprimanded and reminded of her *place*. Each time that happens, I look at her father, who sits quietly on the sidelines. Quite frankly, I think he's afraid of his wife.

Then there's her boyfriend, Tommy. They've been dating since Natalie was fourteen. My mind is blown at the thought of being just shy of twenty-two and having only dated one guy. Her parents thing the sun rises and sets around this guy. But I see right through him, and in my opinion, I think he's a total asshole.

He makes her parents look like a dream. As far as he's concerned, Natalie has absolutely no voice. She's supposed to stand by his side, look pretty, keep her mouth shut, and do as she's told. I've tried to express my concerns, but she won't hear it. This is all she knows. To her, it's normal. Which is a sad reality.

Tommy blew a gasket when he found out she was coming to

Russia for a few weeks with me. That's when I went behind Natalie's back and stepped in. Tommy was sitting on her parents' front porch while Natalie was helping Charlotte make dinner.

"Do you mind if I sit?" I ask and motion to the empty spot on the porch swing.

"Shouldn't you be in the kitchen with the women making dinner?"

"Charlotte and Natalie have it under control," I say sweetly. "I wanted to talk to you."

"About what?" He doesn't bother looking up from his phone.

"About the trip Natalie's taking to Russia."

His head pops up, and he glares at me. "She's not going to Russia."

"There's where you're wrong. Tomorrow morning, we're flying back to JFK, and from there, we're going to St. Petersburg."

"I already told her she's staying here."

"And I'm telling you that's not happening." I stand up and point my finger in his face. "You may be able to silence Natalie, but you can't silence me."

"Who the fuck do you think you are?" Tommy asks, raising his voice. "Natalie belongs to me, and she'll do as I say."

The front door swings open, and Pyotr steps out. "Is there a problem out here?"

"Not at all." I put my hand on Pyotr's arm. "I was just telling Tommy that Natalie and I are leaving for home tomorrow, and he's not standing in the way of our plans."

Tommy stands and gets in my face. "And I was just telling Svetlana to fuck off."

Pyotr steps forward and nudges me out of the way. "I suggest you change your tone, or I'll change it for you."

"Dinner's—" Natalie steps onto the porch and stops mid-sentence as she looks between the three of us. "What's going on?"

"Tommy was just asking what time our flight leaves tomorrow," I say, not breaking eye contact with him. "He didn't know if we needed a ride to the airport."

"My parents are going to drop us off," she responds, taking Tommy's hand. "Do you want to come for the ride to see me off?"

Tommy pulls his hand from hers. "I have plans," he says and walks into the house.

The smile fades from Natalie's face. "He's worried about me going to Russia," she says nervously.

"I'm sure that's all it is," I lie, afraid if I tell her the truth, she'll back out of the trip.

"Dinner's ready."

"We'll be in in a minute."

I wait for Natalie to go inside and ensure she's out of hearing distance before turning to Pyotr. "Can you believe that guy? What a piece of shit."

"He better watch his step tonight. I've about had enough of him."

"Please don't do anything. We just need to get through tonight and get on the plane tomorrow."

Dinner was tense, but that's not out of the ordinary. It's clear Charlotte is as unhappy with my presence as Tommy is. Thankfully, Tommy went home early last night, and according to Natalie, she hasn't heard from him today. In my opinion, that's for the best. Once we land in Russia, I'm hoping she forgets all about him.

After a nearly thirteen-hour flight, the wheels of Papa's jet finally come to a stop on a private airstrip at the Pulkovo Airport. I see a familiar black Escalade parked a short distance away and know my parents are already here. It feels so good to be home.

"I'm nervous," Natalie says between biting her finger nails.

"What for?"

"All of this." She motions out the window. "Until now, New

York City was the furthest I've traveled. I never imagined I'd be in Russia."

I've been trying to get her to come home with me since we first met, but she's always had an excuse why she couldn't. When I was home for the winter break, Papa jumped on our video chat to insist Natalie come stay with us over the summer—to celebrate the end of one journey and the beginning of another. He tends to be pretty insistent, and Natalie was unable to say no. Once we were both back in New York, we worked on getting her a passport so she'd be all ready to travel come summer.

"You're going to love St. Petersburg. Come on." I grab her hand. "I can't wait to see my parents."

Papa's already waiting at the bottom of the steps when the door opens. I hurry down and nearly throw myself at him.

"*Moya babochka*, I have missed you," Papa says while hugging me tight. Unlike many other Eastern European men, he's never been afraid to show emotion or affection.

"I've missed you too."

"Let me look at you." He holds me away from him. "You look well. Happy."

"Thank you. I feel good, too." I look over my shoulder and motion for Natalie to come closer.

"Natalia, it's a pleasure seeing you again," Papa says, surprising her by wrapping her in a hug.

"You as well, Mr. Solonik."

"You must call me Maxim."

"Yes, sir."

The corner of Papa's mouth lifts in a smile. "Come. Let us get you girls home."

While we walk to the car, Pyotr and Misha grab our bags and put them in the back of the SUV.

"Where's Mama?"

"There was an emergency at work."

"Is everything okay?"

"It will be," Papa says as he slides into the front seat.

Once the car is loaded, Misha begins the drive home. It's about an hour before the familiar St. Petersburg sites come into view.

"Svetlana," Natalie says, grabbing my arm. "It's breathtaking."

Tserkov' Spasa na Krovi is lit up, highlighting its iconic onion domes. I didn't realize how much I missed the comforting sights I grew up seeing until they weren't part of the landscape I looked out on every day.

"We'll go see it while we're here. The inside is even more beautiful."

Natalie nods but doesn't look away from the window, watching the beautiful historic architecture that makes up St. Petersburg pass by. As we emerge from the other side of the city, the sights morph into large and equally stunning homes.

Misha slows to a stop at the guard house that sits on the perimeter of our property. The guard on duty gives a slight wave as the tall wrought iron gates open, and Misha drives through.

"Where are we?" Natalie whispers.

"Home."

"You live here?" she asks, eyes wide.

"Yes."

I look at our house and try to see it through Natalie's eyes. A sprawling three-story limestone home sits at the end of a winding driveway. Mahogany double doors are flanked on each side by two pillars. Pristinely manicured greenery lines the front. I've never taken the time to really look at the place I was raised. It's always been just home to me, but for the first time, I see the opulent beauty and realize how lucky I am.

Misha's just shut the car off when the front door flies open, and Mama rushes out. I jump out of the car quickly and run into her embrace.

"I missed you so much."

"Not as much as I missed you." She kisses me on both cheeks. "I'm sorry I didn't make it to pick you up."

"Is everything okay at work?" I ask, concerned.

"It is now." Mama looks over my shoulder and smiles. "Let me go say hello to my other girl." She pulls Natalie in for a hug.

"Thank you so much for inviting me to your home, Mrs. Solonik."

"Irina, please. And we're so glad you're here. Come on in and get settled."

Natalie follows us into the house and lets out a gasp.

"Is everything okay, Natalia?" Papa asks from behind us.

"Your home. I've never seen anything like it."

The foyer is a grand space. The centerpiece is the sweeping Carrara marble staircase that gleams under the light of the crystal chandelier hanging from the high ceiling. At the top of the steps is a balcony. It's one of my favorite spots in our house. On the walls hang centuries-old artwork my parents have collected. The floor is an intricately crafted mosaic made of precious stones, including Jade, Carnelian, Amethyst, Quartz, and Lapis Lazuli.

"It is older than most anything you will find in America."

"Now I'm embarrassed," Natalie says, turning to me.

"Why?"

"For having you stay at our house when you're used to living here."

"Don't be silly. I love going home with you."

I've stayed at Natalie's parents' home several times over the past few years. Natalie says her house is a farmhouse, even though they don't have a proper farm. Something that's always confused me. They do have a relatively large piece of land where Charlotte spends a great deal of time caring for her flower and vegetable gardens during the summer months. Despite the house being older and slightly run down, it's comfortable.

"Come on, I'll show you to your room." I thread my arm through hers and lead her up the staircase.

Brandon

LANA'S PICTURE FLASHES ON MY SCREEN AS THE PHONE rings. "Hello?" I hear her voice a second before the video connects.

"Hi there," Lana says. "I hope I didn't call at a bad time."

"Not at all. Did you just get in?"

"About an hour ago. Papa insisted we have a bite to eat before going to bed." She smiles.

"How did Natalie do?"

"She seems a bit overwhelmed, but I think she'll be okay. It's good for her to get away and see the world."

Although I've yet to meet Natalie, Lana's told me about her parents and boyfriend. I'm not impressed with anything I hear. For people who claim to love her, they're incredibly controlling.

"What time is it there?" I ask.

"Almost two a.m."

"We should keep this short. You must be exhausted."

"Sleep isn't in my near future. My body's all messed up. It thinks I'm still in New York." Lana bites her lip. "I was hoping you and I could spend some time together."

"I see." Even though she's not here, my dick is hard as I imagine the possibilities. "Do you have anything in mind?"

"I do." The camera shakes, and I momentarily have a view of the floor while she props it on the dresser. I travel quite a bit for work, so we've played long-distance plenty of times, but it never grows old.

"Butterfly" by Crazy Town plays in the background, and Lana steps into view. One by one, she sheds each piece of clothing as her hips move to the beat of the music. While I watch her strip tease, I pull my T-shirt over my head and open my pants, freeing my cock. Her hands go to her breasts, kneading the flesh and playing with her nipples. She slides one hand down her toned abdomen to her neatly pussy.

"Are you wet for me?"

Lana's finger disappears between her legs. She drags it languidly along her slit. "Very."

"I wish I was there to taste you." I pump my hand up and down, imagining it's Lana's lips wrapped around me.

Bringing her finger to her mouth, she teases the tip with her tongue like she does to my cock. I groan, wishing it was my mouth on her. She reaches behind her and holds up the purple vibrator we've used in the past when she's been away.

I go to pull the app up and am distracted when I hear a feminine voice in the background.

"Lana, are you awake?"

"Yes. I'll be there in a minute," she calls.

"Who's that?"

"It's Natalie," Lana answers as she grabs a robe and hides the vibrator under her blanket. "I'll call you back."

The call ends, and I drop my head back and groan. Natalie's timing was horrible, but I'm too far gone to stop now. With my free hand, I find the private folder I have on my phone and pull up the video Lana and I made the last time we were together.

Svetlana's spread out over my dining table with my head buried between her legs. I'm eating her like a starving man while my fingers thrust inside her. She's panting and moaning as I bring her to the edge countless times before I curl my fingers inside her, and she explodes on my tongue.

Before her orgasm is finished, I flip her over and pull her feet to the floor. With her bent over, I thrust inside her and fuck her hard and fast. My hand moves, matching my pace on the video until I'm spurting waves of hot cum. It takes the edge off, but my hand is no replacement for Svetlana.

Me: Dream of me, *Mon petit papillon.*

Then, I take a cool shower, hoping to calm my body. Being apart gets more difficult every day.

Svetlana

I ADJUST MY ROBE AND RUN MY FINGERS THROUGH MY hair before I open the door.

"Did I wake you?" Natalie asks.

"No. I was getting ready to take a bath."

"I'm sorry. I'll go back to—"

"It can wait." I step aside. "Come on in. Is everything okay?"

"I don't know." She lets out a frustrated sigh.

"Want to talk about it?" I sit on the bottom of my bed.

"It's Tommy." Natalie joins me. "We just hung up. He's really upset."

"Why?" I resist the urge to roll my eyes.

"Tommy thought we'd get to spend more time together before he had to go back to school."

"You were home for a month, and he was barely around."

"He's been picking up a lot of hours at the pharmacy. He needs the extra money, and Dad plans on having Tommy take it over one day."

If it were anyone other than Natalie, I'd be furious that she's making up excuses for his behavior. The problem is Natalie believes everything she's saying. She's been sheltered all her life—brainwashed, in my opinion. She's learned to accept that she has no voice in her own life. That this is how a healthy relationship works, but she couldn't be further from the truth. Showing her otherwise is a tricky scenario. If I push too much, I'm afraid I'll alienate her, and that's the last thing I want to do.

It's taken years, but Natalie's beginning to loosen up a little. She's gone shopping with me and now owns some more *normal* clothes like jeans and shorter skirts. I even convinced her to go to dinner and a Broadway show with me.

Natalie did well until we returned to Northmeadow at the beginning of summer break. Her demeanor shifted back to mousey, and she left all her new clothes in New York, choosing only to wear ankle-length skirts and blouses that even my *babushka* wouldn't have worn.

"I think he'll survive."

"He was crying."

"Why?"

"Tommy's going back to school next week. Football practice starts. We won't see each other until Thanksgiving."

"He's not even going to be there, and he's giving you a hard time?"

"You don't have a boyfriend. You wouldn't understand." She flops back on my pillow. "Ouch. There's something." Before I can stop her, she's reaching under my blanket. "What's... Oh my God." She holds the silicone dildo in front of her. I grab it and toss it in my top dresser drawer. "Is that what I think it is?" Natalie's cheeks are flaming red.

"It's a sex toy," I say matter-of-factly.

Natalie jumps off the bed and hurries to the door. "I think I should go back to my room."

"You don't have to go."

"I didn't know you had," she hesitates. "That thing."

"There's nothing to be embarrassed about." I try to explain. "It's perfectly normal to have toys and to use them."

"I'll take your word on that. Thank you for the chat, but I

think I should probably try to get some sleep now." She hurries from my room.

"Nat, wait," I say before she gets too far down the hall. She stops and turns around. "There's a whole world out there waiting for you to explore it. Please don't let Tommy hold you back." The words are out of my mouth before I can stop them.

"I'll see you in the morning." Natalie goes into her room, closing the door behind her.

This time, it's me knocking on Natalie's door. "Come in," she calls.

After the way things ended last night, I'm nervous about how things will go today. "Good morning."

"Morning."

"Are you hungry? Breakfast is almost ready."

"I'm starving, actually." Natalie smiles.

"Come on. I'll show you where the kitchen is." We walk down the hallway to a second staircase at the back of the house. "Olga isn't here today, but even when she is, you're more than welcome to go in and grab a snack."

"Who's Olga?"

"She's our chef."

"You have a chef?"

"She not formally trained, but she could outcook any of those people on the American TV cooking shows." I hold the door to the kitchen open. "Here we are."

"Good morning, girls," Mama says as she opens the oven, pulling out a tray.

"Morning," we answer in unison.

"How did you sleep, Natalie?"

"Not the best. You know, the first night in a new place." She shrugs.

"That's understandable." Mama smiles. "I hope you both brought your appetites. I made *Vatrushka* and Lana's favorite, *Syrniki.*"

"I'm not sure what either of those are, but they smell heavenly. Is there anything I can do to help?"

"Would you carry that one to the table?" Mama points to a platter filled with preserves, sweet sour cream, and maple syrup.

"Sure."

Natalie takes the filled platter, and I grab the plate of *Syrniki*. We make our way into the dining room. "Morning, Papa."

"Good morning, *moya babochka.*" He kisses my cheek. "Good morning, Natalia."

"Good morning, mister, I mean, Maxim."

Mama enters the room with the fresh pastries, and we all get settled at the table. One of the ways Mama honors Papa's place as her Dominant is to make his plate before anyone else is served. Natalie watches curiously, and I wonder what she's thinking.

Once Papa's plate is set before him, I don't waste any time grabbing some of the steaming pancakes. "I've missed these so much," I say as I fill my plate. "Our kitchen's very tiny, and the stove hardly works. We end up using the microwave more than I care to admit."

"Then you will be all the more pleased with the surprise I have for you."

"A surprise?"

"In honor of the next step in your educational journey, I've rented an apartment in Greenwich Village for you and Natalia."

"For real?"

"Do I usually joke?"

"Oh my gosh. I can't believe it." I jump up and wrap my arms around his neck. "This is amazing. Isn't it Nat?"

"You didn't have to include me," she says in disbelief.

"We didn't have to. We wanted to." Mama covers Natalie's

hand with hers, giving it a slight squeeze. "You're part of our family now."

"I have already contacted your school and arranged everything with the bursar's office. Your belongings are being moved into your new apartment this week."

"We don't have to live in a tiny dorm anymore," I squeal.

"I don't even know what to say," Natalie adds. "I have no way to repay your kindness."

"Your smile is enough," Papa says.

My parents have visited us in New York on several occasions. Each time, they comment that Natalie always appears nervous. I've told them a little about where she comes from and how she's treated by her parents and boyfriend. It's helped them to better understand why she's so reserved.

"I can't wait to tell my parents."

"You might want to wait on that call. It is the middle of the night for them," Papa chuckles.

"Oh yeah, the time difference. I almost forgot."

While we finish breakfast, Papa shows us pictures of the apartment he has saved on his cell. It has two bedrooms and two and a half bathrooms. It's huge, especially for New York City standards. The recent renovations reflect a sleek and modern style.

Not having to live on campus is something I didn't see coming. I'm surprised and elated that Papa is allowing it. I've put a big focus on personal growth, and I can only hope he sees that I've grown and matured since coming to New York.

Brandon

Celia's muffled screams pierce the darkness, but I can't reach her. I struggle to open my eyes. To chase away the suffocating blackness I'm shrouded in. When I finally pry my lids open, everything around me is fuzzy. Celia's cries are louder—closer.

With painstaking slowness, the scene around me comes into focus, and what I see horrifies me. Angel, Diablo, and several other men I don't recognize huddle around Celia. Some are stroking their erect cocks while they watch the others take their turns with their unwilling victim.

What the hell is wrong with me? I try to move, but my limbs feel like lead weights. My efforts to move them are in vain. I open my mouth to yell something, anything to make them stop, but no sound comes out.

"Hey guys," Angel says, pointing at me. "Look who's awake."

"Now he can watch how a real man fucks a woman," Diablo says, laughing.

Time passes in agonizing increments while I'm trapped in a useless body, watching my girlfriend being tortured. I watch as her head drops. Her cries are no more. It's as though she's resigned herself to her fate. I beg my body to cooperate. First, a finger moves, *then a toe. Little by little, my body and mind become one again, and I pull myself to an upright position.*

"Get the fuck away from her." My voice cracks as I speak. "I said get the fuck away from her."

"What are you planning to do about it?" One of the men says while he thrusts inside Celia.

I sway on my feet and grab the nearest thing to me. Despite my best efforts, I fall to my knees.

"Forget about him," Diablo says. "He won't be interfering any time soon."

Celia turns to look at me. Her beautiful blue eyes are red and swollen from crying, but the fact that she appears miles away scares me. I grab the table and again get to my feet, my legs a little stronger than before. She watches my every move as I reach into my bag and pull out my gun. It's illegal for me to have it in here, but I don't care. I don't leave the house without it. And this is why.

"I'm not going to say it again. Get the fuck away from Celia." I click the safety off. The sound echoes in the small room. The men stop what they're doing and look at one another.

"There's no need for a gun, Brandon," Angel says. "We're just having some fun with her."

"It's not fucking fun when she's not given consent."

"You know what a whore she is. She's loving it." He cackles.

His comment infuriates me. Everything in me itches to pull the trigger. It's only the terrified look on Celia's face that stops me. I don't want to traumatize her any further. "Remove the gag." When no one moves, I yell, "Now."

Angel unbuckles the gag, and it falls to the floor.

"Ask her."

"What are you talking about?"

"Ask her if this is what she wants."

"Come on, Brand. There's no need for this. We'll get our stuff and get out of here." Angel looks at the other men in the room. "Get your things, and let's go." The men, in various stages of undress, replace their clothes.

My hand trembles, but I don't take my finger off the trigger until the last man leaves.

"Brandon," she says my name softly. "I think they hurt the baby." Her head drops as she loses consciousness.

The baby? Reengaging the safety, I rush over to her. "Cece, talk to me," I say as I frantically untie her. "What baby?" Gently, I roll her onto her back. Her bruised body is limp, but it's the blood pooling beneath her that scares me the most. "Fuck." I find my pants and pull out my cell, and dial 911.

"What's your emergency?"

"My girlfriend was assaulted. Raped. She needs your help."

"What's the address?"

I rattle off the address and drop my phone. I find my discarded T-shirt on the floor and carefully pull it over Celia's head. "I'm here, Cece. Everything's going to be okay." I talk to her while I put my pants on. Her eyes don't open. She doesn't stir. "God. Please let her be okay."

It feels like an eternity before the paramedics are pounding on the door. "I'll be right back." I carefully lower her head to the floor to let them in. "She's over here. Hurry, please."

The EMTs crowd around Celia, leaving no room for me. "Is she going to be okay?" No one answers. Their focus is solely on her.

I watch as they load the stretcher into the back of the ambulance. They start to close the doors, and I step forward. "Can I ride with her?"

They look at each other before answering. "I'm sorry. We can only allow family—"

"I'm her fiancé," I interrupt.

"Go ahead," an older male says. "She's going to need a familiar face when she wakes up."

We're halfway to the hospital when her eyes blink open. "Brand?" she asks.

"I'm here, Cece." I jump from my seat, earning a disapproving look from the paramedic who's taking her vitals, and take Celia's hand in mine.

"*Where am I?*"

"*You're in the ambulance on the way to the hospital.*" *Her eyes close once again. I look at the man.* "*Is she okay?*"

"*She's lost a lot of blood.*"

"*You can't leave me,*" *I whisper.* "*Please hang on, Cece.*"

The doctor forces me to wait outside the treatment room while they work to stabilize Celia and collect a rape kit. I pace back and forth in the hall outside her door, praying she's okay. The door opens, and I spin around, but instead of the doctor, it's a female police officer.

"*Are you Ms. Baldwin's fiancé?*" *she asks.*

"*I am.*"

"*And your name is?*"

"*Brandon. Brandon Carpenter.*" *She writes my name in her small notebook.*

"*I'm Officer Weber. I'd like to ask you a few questions.*"

"*Okay. Whatever you need.*"

"*There's a private waiting room down here.*" *She starts walking, but I don't follow.*

"*Can't we talk here? I don't want to leave Celia.*"

"*Brandon,*" *she says softly.* "*This is a sensitive subject that shouldn't be discussed in the hallway. You can come right back to her as soon as we're through.*" *I nod and follow her into the room, where we get settled in the cold and uncomfortable hospital chairs.* "*Can you tell me what you remember from tonight?*"

Tears slip down my face as I recount the details. "*We had a written agreement with Diablo about what would and would not happen tonight. Angel was the only thing we didn't discuss before- hand, but I asked Cece, and she said he could join us.*" *Officer Weber writes down everything I'm saying. Then, I explain what I saw* when I woke up. "I shouldn't have had the beer." I drop my head into my hands.

"How many drinks did you have?"

"One." I look up. "Only one."

"And you blacked out?"

"Yes."

"Would you consent to a blood test?" she asks.

"Yes. I'll do whatever I need to."

"I suspect your drink may have been drugged." She scribbles something in her notebook before continuing. "Can you tell me the names of the men you saw assaulting Ms. Baldwin?"

"Angel Vega and Diablo. Shit." I look at Officer Weber. "I don't know what his real name is."

There's no judgment in her tone when she asks, "Was there anyone else?"

"There were three other men, but I don't know who they were. I've never seen them before."

"Do you know where I can find Mr. Vega and Diablo?"

I give the officer Angel's contact information. "I don't know where to find Diablo. We only communicate when we're at Chains."

"Is there anything else you want to add?"

"I didn't mean for this to happen. I love Celia."

Officer Weber offers me a kind smile. "Let's go find the doctor to get your labs done."

I follow her back down the hall to the nurses' station. She talks quietly with the man there.

"Mr. Carpenter," she says, getting my attention. "This is Bill. He's a physician's assistant and will draw your blood."

"Okay."

"Thank you again for your cooperation," Officer Weber says. "I'll be in touch."

After my lab work, I return to Celia's room and find the door cracked open. I walk in and see Celia awake. A nurse is standing by the bed, checking a monitor.

"Brandon," Celia says my name quietly.

"You're awake." I force a smile as I walk over to her.

"If you need anything, just push the red button," the nurse explains, leaving us alone.

Sitting on the edge of her bed, I take her hand in mine. "How are you feeling?" Tears spill over her eyelids. "Don't cry, Cece."

"I'm so sorry, Brand," her voice cracks.

"There's nothing for you to apologize for."

"I was pregnant. I was going to tell you after our scene tonight. But I lost the baby." Celia's body is wracked with sobs. "I'm so sorry."

Pregnant.

A baby.

Our baby.

"Please say something," Celia begs, but no words come. I'm in shock, trying to process what she said. "Are you mad at me?"

"No," I say quickly and take her face in mine. "I could never be mad at you."

"I just found out. I was going to tell you. I promise. I wanted it to be a surprise," she says without taking a breath.

"Shh. It's okay."

"I'm sorry to interrupt," the doctor says as he enters the room. "I was able to reach your parents. They're on their way, but I don't want to wait to take you to the OR."

"The OR?"

The doctor pulls up a chair as he patiently explains everything. "Celia is still bleeding heavily. Part of that is from the trauma of the assault. I also suspect there is remaining tissue in her uterus." Celia clings to my hand. "She and I discussed taking a wait-and-see approach or having the procedure."

"I opted for the surgery," she says quietly.

"Is it dangerous?"

"It's a fairly routine procedure. Like any surgery, there are risks, but they're minimal."

"I'll be okay, Brandon. Will you wait here for my parents?"

"Yes, of course."

"*Are you ready?*" *She nods.* "*We'll be back in a minute to take you to the OR.*"

We only have a minute before several nurses enter the room. Everything happens quickly as they transfer Celia to a portable stretcher and push her out of the room.

I stand in the hallway helplessly as I watch them wheel Celia away from me.

Brandon

Work has been nothing short of torturous this morning. My mind focuses more on Svetlana than the accounts in front of me. Which is why I'm shocked when I finish typing this email and find I'm caught up on everything.

Me: Are you busy?

Alex: No, why?

Me: I'll be over in a min. I need to talk to you.

Lana and I have been dating one another, but we've not made any further steps toward a Dominant/submissive dynamic, and I'd like that to change. I'm ready to take the next step and begin vetting each other. I've written up a loose outline for a contract. I'm hoping she and I can discuss it and take the next step toward becoming an official Dom/sub couple.

I grab the manilla folder and cut through the conference room to Alex's office.

While he looks over the document, I sit on his couch, tapping my fingers on my leg. "What do you think?"

"It's a good starting point," he says as he finishes the last page. "It should be fine."

"Good."

"I thought you didn't want another dynamic. What made you change your mind?"

Since we first met, so much has changed in my life and Lana's. She's the first woman I've ever opened up to about what happened that night with Celia. I was certain Lana would be disgusted and walk away, but she didn't. She cried with me for Celia and everything we lost that night. Instead of putting a wedge between us, it brought us closer together.

I still had to face a hurdle but didn't know how.

"I bumped into Celia a few months ago," I confess.

"I thought she left town."

"She did. She and her husband flew in from Texas to visit her parents."

"Her husband?" Alex lifts his eyebrow. "How did that go?"

It's late, and I'm hungry. I don't want to cook, so I walk the few blocks to get a tray of Krispy's pizza. I'm distracted watching a video on my cell while I pull the restaurant's door open.

"Brandon?"

The familiar voice steals the breath from my lungs.

"Celia? What are you doing here?"

"We're visiting my parents." I look behind her and spot a tall man holding a sleeping baby close to his chest. "Brandon, this is my husband, Donovan."

"It's nice to meet you," Donovan says. "I've heard a lot about you."

That can't be good. Part of me wants to turn and run.

"Van, do you mind going back without me. I want to talk to Brandon."

"Sure." He kisses her cheek and walks away.

"I should've asked you first," she says. "Do you mind company?"

"Not at all." My eyes follow her husband as he disappears around the corner. "You have a baby."

"Clover's our youngest. We also have a two-year-old boy, Jax." Pain squeezes my heart like a vice. *"I'm sorry. I didn't mean to upset you."*

"You haven't." I manage a small smile. "Do you want to walk to the park?"

"Didn't you come here to eat?"

I suddenly have no appetite. "It can wait."

Celia and I walk a few blocks in silence. I haven't seen her in over ten years, but she hasn't changed. She's still petite with long, silky black hair and eyes that are the color of the sky on a cloudless day. So many thoughts go through my mind, but I can't voice any of them.

"How have you been?" she asks when we get to the park entrance.

"I'm well. How about you?"

"I'm doing good."

We continue further to the other side of the park, where there's a lone bench. In front of us, the water from Gravesend Bay laps onto the rocky shore. Off to one side, the Verazzano Bridge lights up the evening sky. When we were teenagers, we spent so much time sitting here. Celia would curl up against my side while we dreamt about our future together. The future we didn't get to have.

"How are your parents?" I ask as we sit.

"Mom's doing well. Dad, not so much." She looks down at her hands folded in her lap. "He was diagnosed with cancer."

"I didn't know that. Is it bad?"

"Yes," she says quietly. "It's pancreatic cancer, but it's metasta-sized to his bones."

"What can I do?" I ask, instinctively reaching for her hand but pulling away at the last second. I'm no longer a high school kid with no resources. I make more money than I can spend. "I'll have a doctor brought in to consult on—"

"That's very kind." Celia touches my arm. "Donovan already had a colleague review his case. There's nothing that can be done."

"Your husband's a doctor?"

"He's a pediatric neurosurgeon."

"I see."

"That's why we came in. Dad doesn't have much time left."

"I'm so sorry, Cece."

"*No one's called me that in a very long time.*" *We sit silently for several seconds before she asks, "Are you married?"*

"*No,*" *I answer quickly. "I don't think I'm marriage material.*"

"*Why would you say something like that?*"

"*You, of all people, know the answer to that.*"

"*Brandon, you are not responsible for what happened that night." I get up and walk a few steps away. Celia follows and moves to stand in front of me. "You were as much a victim as me." I shake my head. She reaches out and touches my face with her hand. "Bran, look at me, please." I shift my gaze down to her. "I don't blame you for anything that happened. You need to stop blaming yourself and move forward.*"

"*How can you say that?*"

"*Because I know you're a good man. We were both young and stupid—and we paid a steep price for our foolishness.*"

"*I was supposed to protect you.*"

"*And you did.*"

"*After you were hurt doesn't count.*"

"*Of course, it counts. I would've died in that room if it wasn't for you.*"

"*Things would be so different today if I hadn't—*"

"*Shh." Celia places her delicate finger against my lips. "We're exactly where we're supposed to be right now.*"

Instinctively, I wrap my arms around her tiny frame and pull her against my chest. She doesn't resist. Instead, she puts her arms around me and rests her head against my body. Lowering my face, I kiss the top of her head. Her hair still smells like strawberries. I close my eyes and allow the happy memories of our past to wash over me, remembering all the other times I held her in this exact spot.

"*I've missed the feel of your arms around me," Celia says, her voice catching on a sob.*

"*Does he treat you well?" I ask, tears trailing down my face.*

"*He does. Donovan loves me and is a good father to our children.*"

All these years, I've worried that Celia had to live with the memory of being raped. Of knowing the life she carried inside her died in that room. "Are you happy?"

"I am." She looks up at me. "But a piece of my heart has always been yours. It will always belong to you."

"And mine yours." I hear footsteps and spin around, pulling Celia protectively behind me.

"Sorry, I didn't mean to startle you," Donovan says with his hands up.

"What are you doing here?" Celia asks, stepping out from my protective hold.

"I didn't want you walking back in the dark by yourself. Your mom said I'd probably find you here." He looks between the two of us. "Is everything okay?"

"It is." I attempt to reassure him.

"Clover's starting to fuss. She's getting hungry," he explains. "Are you ready to go?"

"Give me one more minute."

"Sure." Donovan walks away, giving us a few more minutes of privacy.

"I'm glad we bumped into each other," Celia says. "Can I give you my number so we can keep in touch?"

"I can't— I don't think that's a good idea, Cece. I can't be in your life and not be with you." I glance over to where Donovan is waiting for his wife. "There's someone I met a while ago. I've been holding back, but I think now's the time to take the next step with her."

"I understand," Celia says, using the backs of her hands to wipe her face. "Whoever the woman is. She's very lucky to have your heart." Then, she stands on her tiptoes and gently kisses my cheek before she turns and goes to her husband.

He says something quietly to her. She nods and threads her fingers with his. They walk away, leaving me standing there, alone.

"I'm glad you saw her," Alex says. "Hopefully, now that she's told you the same things we've been saying for years, you'll listen."

"You're one to talk." Alex has sworn off relationships and love.

"We're not here to talk about me." He holds up the contract. "This is about you and Lana."

"Right," I chuckle. "I'll talk to her when she comes back from visiting her parents."

"That's a great idea."

Lana hasn't brought up the idea of a contract since we met, and for a long time, that was okay with me. I was living in the past and drowning in guilt. There was so much that was wrong about that night at Chains. Things I had no idea about at the time.

It wasn't until I met Alex and started going to Fire and Ice that I learned about the BDSM lifestyle for what it really is. What I experienced there was the complete opposite of everything I saw and did at Chains. I've always been a Dominant but feared making a lasting commitment.

That chance meeting with Celia was something I desperately needed. She is the only one who was able to grant me true forgiveness. The kind I needed to forgive myself. That night marked a new beginning for me as a Dominant.

Svetlana

Pʏᴏᴛʀ ᴛʀᴀɪʟs ʙᴇʜɪɴᴅ Nᴀᴛᴀʟɪᴇ ᴀɴᴅ ᴍᴇ ᴀs ᴡᴇ sightsee in St. Petersburg. Today, we're spending the afternoon at The State Hermitage Museum. It's the second-largest art museum in the world and has over three million pieces in its collection. I haven't been here since I was a schoolgirl, so I'm enjoying it as much as Natalie.

"Your parents are wonderful," she says. "They're still so much in love with each other, and they're so easy to talk to. I wish my parents were more like them."

"I'm fortunate to have been raised with their example." Their relationship is the model for what I hope to have one day.

"I hope one day Tommy looks at me like your father looks at your mother," Natalie says wistfully. "I guess that's something that comes with time."

"Did you ever consider that Tommy might not be the right one?" I ask without taking my eyes off the painting on the wall.

"What do you mean?"

"Maybe you should go on a few dates while you're away at school?"

"That would be cheating." Natalie looks horrified.

"Not if you tell him you're doing it," I explain. "Tommy's the only guy you've ever dated. I know you plan on marrying him, but I think you should get some more experience before you take that step."

"I can't believe you're saying this." She picks up the pace of her walking.

"I didn't mean to upset you," I say as I catch up to her.

"What did you think my reaction would be?"

"I hoped you'd see reason."

"Tommy loves me. We've never dated anyone else, and I'm just fine with keeping it that way."

"You're positive he's not seeing anyone while he's away at school?"

"Of course, he isn't. He'd never cheat on me."

"I'm sorry. I don't want to fight about Tommy or upset you."

"I love him, Lan. And he loves me."

"The only thing that really matters is that you're happy."

"I am." Natalie smiles.

"Then, I'm happy." I link my arm with hers, and we walk to the next exhibit.

I'm far from an expert on relationships. Lord knows I've done my fair share of screwing up in that department. I guess I should be happy she's seeing an example of a healthy relationship. Hopefully, it's something she'll continue to think about and compare it to her relationship with Tommy.

Natalie's enjoying time in the sun by the outdoor pool while I'm in my room. Everyone suspects I've come up to call a guy. And it is, but not the way they all think. In reality, my phone call is to have a long-distance session with my therapist, Grayson.

After a particularly loud and intense fight with Alex, Star pulled me aside for a heart-to-heart talk about my attitude. At first, I was defensive, assuming she was going to tell me why I was wrong and why Alex was right. That was part of the conversation because, like it or not, Alex was right. But instead of lecturing me, she told me a story about a submissive she knew many years ago.

The girl was gorgeous, which attracted the attention of many Dominants. But every dynamic she entered ended in failure. The problem—the girl could never get her attitude under control. She was disrespectful to all of her Dominants, making them look bad in front of the rest of the community. She didn't respond to their correction and was always released. Several experienced Domme's and submissives approached her, trying to mentor her. They wanted to see her succeed, but she wouldn't take advice from anyone. In the end, she walked away from the lifestyle.

Star told me I reminded her so much of that girl. That I have a lot of potential to be a good submissive, but I need to work on myself. She explained that before I could submit to a Dominant in a meaningful way, I needed to be strong and confident in myself.

Her words struck a chord in my heart, and I let my guard down enough to take the constructive advice. She put me in touch with a kink-friendly therapist, something I'd never heard of. I called him the next day and started therapy that week. The twist is I didn't tell Alex or Brandon anything about it. Not because I was ashamed or wanted to hide it, though.

The last time I spoke to Masha, she opened my eyes to the fact that I never truly let my guard down when I saw her. Because of that, I didn't make any real progress toward the goals we set. This time, I promised myself I'd be completely honest with my therapist and, most importantly, myself. My hope was the people around me would eventually see a change. And that's exactly what's happened.

About six months after I started my sessions, Alex removed his collar of protection.

When I get to Alex's house, I'm surprised to find him sitting on his sofa. "What are you doing here?"

"I live here."

"Very funny. You know what I mean."

"I left the office early. I want to do something before we go to the club tonight." He pats the couch. "Come sit down."

"Okay," I say hesitantly as I take a seat.

"We've gotten to know one another quite well. Don't you agree?" Alex asks.

"Yes."

"When you first came, I seriously doubted if we'd make it until you moved into the dorm. When you did, the oddest thing happened."

I wait for him to tell me, but he says nothing. "Well, what happened?"

"I missed having you around." He laughs, and I join him. "You've come a long way from the impulsive and argumentative girl you were."

"Thank you. I think."

Alex takes a deep breath. "It's time to remove your collar."

His words shock me, and my hand instinctively reaches for the chain around my neck. Why?"

"You no longer need it."

When Alex first put his collar around my neck, I thought I'd suffocate under its weight. I hated it and wanted to tear it off, but I knew if I did, Papa would find out, and I'd be on his jet returning to Russia. But now I've grown used to it—like it even. The thought of being without it is scary. "What do you mean? Aren't you supposed to be protecting me? I don't have a Dominant—"

"Svetlana," Alex interrupts me. "You no longer need the collar. That doesn't change the fact that I'll always be your friend and will be the first, well maybe the second in line, to protect you."

I carry Alex's collar with me all the time. It's a physical reminder that I'm never alone.

That night, Alex said he noticed a new sense of maturity and complimented the personal growth I showed both in and out of the club. At that point, I confided in him about going to therapy. The look of pride on his face is something I'll never forget.

"Svetlana," Gray says when the video connects. "How are you?"

"I'm doing well. Thanks for asking."

"Are you enjoying your trip home?"

"I am. I didn't realize how much I missed it here. Being around familiar sights and sounds is really nice."

"Is there anything specific you'd like to address today?" Gray always gives me a choice as to how the session will proceed.

"Brandon asked me again about introducing him to my friends."

"What did you say?"

"I told him I wasn't ready yet."

"Can you help me understand your reasoning?" he asks and jots something down.

"I like to keep my circle small, so I don't feel they need to know that much about me."

"That's fair."

"And part of me is embarrassed."

"Why?" he asks with genuine curiosity.

"I think Brandon thinks I'm some popular girl with tons of friends. I don't know what he'll think if he finds out that, with the exception of Natalie, there's no one else."

"Do you really think he'll care?" I shrug. "From everything you've told me about Brandon, I don't think the quantity of your friends is important."

"Even if he doesn't, Natalie is a whole other kind of issue."

"What does he know about her?" Gray asks.

"We've discussed Natalie. He knows I love her dearly, and she's my closest friend. I've explained that she grew up sheltered. Let me correct that, *very* sheltered." I fill Gray in on my latest visit to Northmeadow and explain exactly how naïve Natalie is. "I know Brandon and I aren't a Dom/sub couple, at least not yet. But I have no explanation for how we met, and I don't want to keep anything else from her. There's enough as it is."

"There's a lot to explore there. Which of those issues do you want to cover first?"

I really don't want to discuss the things I keep from Natalie, so I opt for talking about the pros and cons of a Dom/sub dynamic with Brandon. "He hasn't said anything about it in a long time, but I can feel it coming, and I don't want to be left unprepared if and when that conversation comes up."

"How does that make you feel?"

Whenever I think about submitting to Brandon, it brings up a lot of feelings about Slava and what happened between us. Things I thought I'd resolved within myself. "I just remember feeling so constricted. Like I'd suffocate in the shadow of a Dominant. Does that make sense?"

"It does. Why do you think you feel that way?"

Sometimes, I wish Gray would give me the answers instead of making me try to figure them out. "I don't know."

"I think if you allow yourself to reflect on the situation, you'll find your answer."

"Maybe I'm not made to settle down with just one person?" I shrug.

"What makes you say that?"

"I have to think that if I was supposed to be with one person, I wouldn't have reservations about it. That I'd look forward to submitting to a Dominant rather than fear it."

Gray pauses before speaking. "I hear what you're saying, but I think you're confusing two different things."

"How so?"

"Submitting to a Dominant in this lifestyle and choosing a life mate are not one and the same," he explains. "Signing a contract is not a life sentence, if you will. It doesn't have to signify the end of your freedom but the beginning of the next amazing adventure. You're also only looking at a dynamic from your point of view."

"What do you mean?"

"When Slava wanted to negotiate another contract, instead of talking with him, you imagined what you thought he wanted and how the conversations would go. You didn't allow him to tell you his thoughts."

"I don't want to make those same mistakes with Brandon."

"I know you don't," he says with a smile. "Unfortunately, we're out of time for today. I'd like you to take some time to explore those thoughts this week. Perhaps you'll view this situation and Brandon in a new light."

"I'll do that."

"And Lana."

"Yes?"

"You avoided the whole part about Natalie. We'll talk about that next week."

"I'll hold you to that." We share a laugh.

After we hang up, I take my time changing into my swimsuit. What Gray touched on has me thinking about my feelings for Brandon. I have a great time with him, and our chemistry is off the charts. The sex is some of the best I've had. Gray's right, though. I'm doing exactly what I did with Slava. We haven't had any serious conversations about what a dynamic between us might look like. Yet, I'm assuming what his answers will be. I need to not put the proverbial horse before the cart.

There are also questions I feel I need to ask myself, such as do I want to settle down with one man? Are marriage and children something I see in my future? If and when Brandon and I have those conversations, I want to know what my answers are so neither of us is left with unrealistic expectations.

There's so much going on in my head right now. Fortunately for me, I'll be in Russia for the next few weeks, so I don't have to make any decisions today.

Brandon

I'M LEAVING THE GYM WHEN I GET A TEXT FROM ALEX.

Alex: Max's jet landed a few minutes ago. Pyotr's dropping Natalie off at the dorm before bringing Lana to my house.

Me: Thanks for the update.

Alex: You're welcome to stop over this evening.

Me: I think I'll give her a few days to settle in.

Alex: Whatever you think is best.

And that's the problem. I have no damn clue what's best. I sat down with Star and Owen earlier this week to get their opinions on the contract. Owen pointed out a few details he felt should be added due to Lana's and my past that I overlooked. The most critical part was discussing potential triggers that either of us was aware of. He also suggested I add a spot for Lana to tell me her fantasies because that's a great way to create role-play scenes. I left Fire and Ice confident with the contract.

Lana: Hey. I'm back in town. Care for some company tonight?

Me: Welcome back. I have plans tonight.

Lana: Are those plans going to take *all* night?

Me: Unfortunately, they are.

Lana: Oh.

Me: Maybe we can get together during the week?
Lana: I'll see what my schedule looks like.
Me: Ok. Talk later.

Before Lana and I go any further, we need to talk—with our clothes on. I'm looking for something long-term with Svetlana, hopefully, a relationship that will continue to grow outside of any contractual dynamic we establish. I don't want to get into this tonight when she's just returned from a long plane ride and will undoubtedly be jet-lagged. With so much on the line, I feel it's important we take the time to discuss every aspect of a Dom/sub relationship. I need to know what kind of a submissive she is, and she needs to know that I'm capable of being her Dominant.

I've learned a lot since everything that happened with Celia. I've trained under experienced Dominants and am surrounded by responsible people who practice the BDSM lifestyle. Those who know about my past remind me I'm not the same person I was in my early twenties. Sure, I'm human, and mistakes happen, but I have knowledge now that I did not have back then.

After Celia's rape, Chains was shut down. The two men, who I didn't know then, are each serving a fifteen-year-sentence for rape in the first degree. Angel is serving a twenty-five-year sentence for rape in the first degree and additional charges for drugging me.

Diablo, the mastermind behind their plan, is serving thirty years. He was charged with rape in the first degree, false imprisonment, and a slew of other offenses. The trial for him was brutal, especially for Celia. Sitting in the courtroom, watching her on the stand reliving the most horrifying night of her life, was gut-wrenching.

When Diablo took the stand, he was so sure he'd be off the hook since we'd done other scenes together that he forgot this time we had a written contract. It was the first time Celia was going to be whipped. After searching online for some guidelines, I read that we should have everything in writing, just in case. That way, there'd be no confusion about what is acceptable or not. Included in that was that I was to be present at all times. Celia was not to be gagged or otherwise restricted from using speech, and no one else would be included without Celia and my prior consent. Diablo's signature was on that paper, alongside ours, showing he understood and agreed to the very rules he broke.

It was vindication to see them escorted from the courtroom in handcuffs, knowing they'd each be spending a good number of years in jail. But at the same time, it did little to bring back the life that was taken from us.

After the trial concluded, Celia's parents whisked her from the courtroom. Her attorney approached me before I could catch up to them with a request from Mr. and Mrs. Baldwin to have no further contact with Celia. He informed me she would be relocating to a small town in Texas with a family member. Despite how much their request broke me, I agreed. I didn't want to cause Celia any more pain. That was the last time I saw her until we bumped into one another a few months ago.

Our chance meeting came at the perfect time. Having the opportunity to talk to her gave me the closure I never had. It was the missing piece I needed to feel confident moving ahead with Svetlana.

Svetlana

"Yes. Why?"

"You're gripping your phone so tight it looks like you're going to break it," Natalie says.

I loosen my hold. "Everything's good."

Pyotr pulls up in front of our new apartment. "The building's beautiful. I can't wait to see the apartment." Natalie smiles and gets out of the car. When I don't follow, she bends over and looks into the car. "Are you coming?"

"Actually, no. I'm staying at my friend's place for a few days."

"Maybe I should stay in the dorm then?"

"Don't be silly. Go ahead and get settled. I'll be back later in the week."

"Are you sure?" she asks uncertainly.

"Positive." I smile, trying to reassure her.

"Okay, I guess."

Pyotr waits until Natalie is inside before pulling away. "I thought you were going to Brandon's?" he asks.

"So did I, but apparently, he has *other* plans tonight," I say through gritted teeth.

"I see." Pyotr's response is clipped.

70

The rest of the drive is silent as I will myself not to cry.

Me: I hope you don't mind. I'm on my way to your place.

Alex: That's not a problem, but I thought you'd be anxious to see your new apartment.

Me: I was anxious to see Brandon, but he's unavailable tonight. Do you know where he is?

Alex: Nope. It is not my weekend to Brandon-sit

Me: Your comedian skills need work. Don't quit your day job.

Alex: I'll be at the office late. See you later.

Between being one of Manhattan's top marketing firms and all the stuff Papa sends his way, Alex's going to work his way into an early grave.

I pace back and forth in front of the floor-to-ceiling windows overlooking the river while I obsess over Brandon's text. He has plans for tonight—all night. I've gone from hurt to mad to furious. "I'm not sitting here while he does whatever he's doing with another woman tonight." I decide there's no way I'm just going to sit here tonight.

I shower quickly and, with a towel wrapped around me, take my time drying my hair so it hangs long and silky down my back. I apply my makeup, making sure I have smoky eyes and sexy red lipstick. My dorm was too small to bring all my clothes, something I'm thankful for now as I find the dress I'm looking for.

The satin fabric is cool against my skin. The front of the dress has a plunging cowl neck. Halter ties allow for a backless design. The bottom of the dress hits mid-thigh and features a sexy slit that leaves very little to the imagination. Stiletto heels complete my look.

I take the elevator down to Viktor's apartment, where Pytor stays while I'm here. I find him chilling on the couch watching television. "Pyotr, do you mind driving me to Brandon's?"

"I thought he had plans?"

"He does."

"Did you let Alex know?"

"I'll send him a text on the way."

We hit the rush hour traffic from all the commuters making their mass exodus from the city for the weekend, which makes the ride to Brooklyn take forever. The subway would've been much faster, but Pyotr isn't a huge fan.

Finally, we're in Brandon's neighborhood. "Don't pull in his driveway. I don't want him to know I'm here."

"Are you sure you know what you're doing?"

"I'm positive," I lie. Because, in reality, I don't know if I can handle what I'll find when I walk into his house.

"Did you text Alex?"

Just sent it. I hold up the phone.

Me: I dropped my stuff off at your place. I decided to go out. Don't wait up for me.

"Can you wait out here?"

"I'd rather come in."

"I doubt this will take long."

"If you're not out in fifteen minutes, I'm coming in."

"Deal."

For a brief second, I almost let my nerves get the best of me. I pause and look back to where Pyotr is waiting in the car, but I can't back out. With my key in hand, I pull my shoulders back and unlock the door.

Other than a small light, the downstairs is dark. I hear music coming from upstairs and walk in that direction. Once I'm upstairs, I walk toward Brandon's room, where the music is coming from. His door is closed. My stomach turns as I reach out to turn his doorknob.

"I hope I'm not interrupting your other plans," I say as I open his bedroom door.

Brandon

"ARE YOU STILL AT WORK?" I ANSWER MY RINGING phone.

"I just got a text from Pyotr," Alex says.

"Is everything okay?"

"Did something happen between you and Lana?"

"Not that I'm aware of. She called earlier and asked about getting together tonight."

"What did you tell her?"

"I told her I had plans tonight." I pause as the realization hits me. "Lana must've thought I meant with another woman."

"Where are you?"

"I'm at home."

"Why did you tell her you had plans tonight?"

"I knew if she came over tonight, we wouldn't get any talking done. I wanted to wait until we could discuss a contract and vetting."

"She just got back in town after being away for over a month."

"I'm very aware of that."

Pyotr: What the fuck are you up to, Carpenter?

"I have to go." I don't wait for Alex to say goodbye before I hang up.

Me: I think there was a misunderstanding.

Pyotr: Oh?

Me: I told Lana I had plans tonight, but it's not what she thinks.

Pyotr: Keep talking.

Me: I want to take our relationship to the next level and officially become her Dominant, but I didn't want to do it tonight. I wanted to let her get settled in after her trip.

Pyotr: Are you alone?

Me: Of course.

Pyotr: Good, because she's on her way in, and I didn't want to have to kill you.

I'd laugh if I didn't think Pyotr was serious. I'm well aware that if I did something to fuck up and Lana got hurt, my life may very well be on the line.

I hurry out of the bathroom, still wet from my shower, and look out my window. Sure enough, Lana's walking up the steps to my house. I can only imagine what she's expecting to find. I only have seconds to throw a pair of pants on and get out of my room.

She's downstairs, so I move quickly and quietly. Her heels click on the hardwood floors as she walks past the guestroom on her way to my bedroom.

"I hope I'm not interrupting your other plans," she says, and I hear the door hit the wall. "Brandon?"

Quietly, I come up behind her. "Yes?"

She jumps and spins around to face me. "Where is she?"

"Where is who?"

"Your *plans.*" She puts her hands on her hips.

"There's no one here but me."

"Mhm." She lifts an eyebrow.

"Feel free to check." I motion with my hand.

"I think I will." She purposely nudges me with her elbow as she storms by.

While she throws open the doors to the guestrooms, I lean

against my doorframe with my arms crossed. I'm enjoying watching her in the sexy little dress she's wearing.

When she gets to the last door, she turns around. "There isn't anyone here."

"I know."

"You said you had plans," she says quietly.

"I wanted you to settle in and get a good night's sleep." I push off the wall. "Because I knew when I saw you the last thing you were going to get to do is rest."

"Why didn't you just say that?" She swallows.

"I didn't choose my words wisely."

"I thought you were spending the night with someone else."

"Why would you ever think that?"

"I've been gone all summer, and I guess I assumed—"

"I love you, Svetlana." I blurt out, cutting her off.

She freezes, her eyes wide. "You love me?"

"Yes." I take a step closer, closing the distance between us. "I love you." My mouth crashes into hers, and I thread my fingers through her hair. "You are mine," I say between breaths. "Do you understand?"

"I do."

"I need to hear you say it."

"I'm yours, Brandon."

Hearing those words sparks something inside me. I lift her, and she wraps her legs around my waist as I carry her back into my bedroom, where I kick the door closed behind us.

Lana unhooks her legs, and I slide her down my body. "Strip for me."

Svetlana

Brandon morphed from his usual sweet demeanor into a jealous alpha male. When I got here, I was furious with him, thinking he was cheating on me. I made a total fool of myself, checking his house like he was hiding another woman. But then something in him changed. A switch flipped, and my misplaced anger transitioned into intense arousal. I've never had a man go crazy possessive over me. I love it.

"Strip for me," Brandon commands.

Slowly, I lower the zipper on the side of my dress. The satin fabric slips off my body as it billows to the floor. I'm left standing completely nude.

Brandon steps toward me, and I instinctively move back until I'm against the bed and fall onto it. He spreads my legs and pushes them apart, stopping to look at me like I'm a feast about to be eaten. Then, his head lowers, and he runs his tongue along my slit. It's a slow and languid movement. "I need more." I squirm, trying to encourage him, but it has the opposite effect.

"Stay still," he says, grabbing my hips. I whimper in protest, and he looks up at me. "Are you going to be obedient?"

"Yes." He raises an eyebrow, and I know what he's silently asking. Although we don't have a contract or any kind of official dynamic, Brandon's always been a Dominant in the bedroom. "Yes, Sir. I'll stay still."

Then, his head disappears between my thighs again, his tongue skillfully caressing every inch. He dances between passionate caresses and rough intensity, eliciting a symphony of sensations that leave me breathless and yearning for release. With each flick and tease of his tongue, I find myself on the precipice of bliss, panting and whispering fervent pleas for him to grant me the sweet surrender of ecstasy.

"I love hearing you beg," he says.

"Please." My voice is barely above a whisper.

"Please, what?" He looks up with a grin on his face.

"I need—" My eyes close as he spears two fingers inside me. "Yes, that."

"Is this what you want?" I nod, and he stills.

"Yes. And your mouth." Oh God, I need his mouth on me.

"You're a greedy girl, aren't you?"

"I am. I want all of you, please, Brandon."

Without warning, his mouth envelops my sensitive bud. I'm overwhelmed by the intense sensations. His skilled fingers thrust in and out, propelling me toward the precipice of desire. In a swirling whirlwind of ecstasy, I lose myself completely. My body arches as euphoric waves crash over me. Lost in my pleasure, I am oblivious to Brandon removing his clothes until he thrusts inside me.

"Fuck, Svetlana." He holds my hips tight. "I missed you."

"I missed you, too."

"I need you to listen to me. I would never cheat on you. No one could capture my heart and soul the way you have. From the moment our paths crossed, it's been you. It'll always be you. Do you understand?"

"I understand."

He keeps up his punishing rhythm, and my body tenses as another orgasm builds from deep inside.

"Let yourself fall, *papillion*. I'll catch you."

I've never had a man claim me the way Brandon is right now. It's as if he's marking me as his own. I can't hold back any longer. The overwhelming surge of pleasure becomes too much to contain, and an explosive orgasm radiates from the core of my being. As my body convulses around his rigid length, it triggers his release. His eyes squeeze shut, and his head falls backward as he surrenders to the intensity of our connection.

"If getting jealous causes this, maybe I should let it happen more often," I giggle.

His head snaps up, and he pulls out. "I'm not joking, Svetlana."

"Me either." I push up on my elbows. "I like this side of you."

"We need to talk," Brandon says, picking up his T-shirt and passing it to me. "Get dressed." He slides his legs into his jeans while I pull his shirt over my head. "I'll be right back," he says, disappearing from the room.

I sit cross-legged on the bed, waiting for him to return. When he does, he has a manilla folder in his hand. "What's that?"

"This is why I wanted to wait until another day."

"What is it?" I crane my neck, trying to see what's inside, but he holds it just out of sight.

Brandon

THIS IS NOT HOW I PLANNED TO HAVE THIS conversation. Hearing Lana mention the possibility of me being with another solidified my decision to do this tonight. I've never experienced such a fierce sense of possession and desire for a woman as I do for Lana. She's mine, and mine alone. Tonight, I intend to deepen that connection between us.

"I'd like to discuss a contract," I say, gauging Lana's reaction.

"You would?" she asks.

"Yes."

"When did you change your mind?"

"I told you this is what I wanted when I met you, but I had a few personal hurdles to overcome before I felt ready to begin negotiating a contract." I sit on the bed beside Lana. "We need to discuss my past. The reason I've been holding off on doing this."

My hands tremble as I tell Lana about Celia. It's uncomfortable recounting this part of my past. But I can't move forward with a Dom/sub relationship without being completely transparent about one of my biggest regrets and most important life lessons. Svetlana listens quietly, her features giving nothing away as to what she might be thinking or feeling as I lay everything at her feet.

"For years, I've replayed that night in my head, wishing I'd done things differently and berating myself for not coming to sooner. There's been times I imagined I'd pulled the trigger." My voice cracks, and I pause to regain control of my emotions. "I bumped into Celia a few months ago. It was the first time we've spoken since then. All these years, I assumed she hated me, but I was wrong. She never blamed me for what happened."

"Why would she?"

"Because I failed her."

"You saved her," Lana says, wiping a stray tear from my cheek. "How is she today?"

"She's happily married and has two children." I smile. "Celia encouraged me to forgive myself and to be happy."

"She's right. There was nothing you could've done differently—"

"Yes, there was. I should've asked more questions and learned more about BDSM before we went to a club and especially before I allowed anyone to play with us. That will never happen again."

"You aren't open to playing with other people?"

"No," I answer without hesitation. "I will not share you with anyone. That's a hard limit for me."

"May I see the contract?" she asks. I pull out her copy and pass it to her, watching her read. "You know how to use a whip?" she asks.

"I do. But if that's not something you're interested in, we can put it on the hard limit list."

"Don't take it out. I'm very interested in it," she says, smiling.

"Do you have any experience being whipped?" I'm curious to learn more about Svetlana as a submissive.

"A little, yes, and I liked it very much."

"I take it you're willing to begin vetting and negotiating a contract?" Lana bites her lip as she looks between the papers and me but says nothing. "Tell me what you're thinking."

She sets the papers on the bed in front of her. "I feel like I'm at a crossroads. This is what I've wanted for so long, and I want to say yes."

"But?"

"I'm scared. I don't want to ruin what we have."

"I'm terrified, too."

Over the past two years, Lana and I have gotten to know each other, and we've had a lot of fun dating, but something's always been missing—being an official Dominant and submissive couple. We have a good sex life full of kink, but that does not encompass the totality of what the BDSM lifestyle offers.

After I started going to Fire and Ice, I had a submissive for a short time. Owen introduced me to Wynter, an experienced submissive. We got along well and, after a period of vetting, signed a contract. My relationship with her allowed me to practice my fledging skills with someone who wouldn't let me go too far. Was it a conventional Dom/sub dynamic? Probably not. But that's the beauty of this lifestyle. It's not a one-size-fits-all kinda thing. Wynter and I designed a dynamic that met our needs and provided her with the safety net I insisted be built in.

We ended the dynamic when Wynter's job offered her a transfer to Finland. It was an opportunity that was too good for her to pass up. She asked me to go with her, but I wasn't willing to walk away from my life here. It wasn't easy to release her, but our dynamic ended on good terms.

Since then, I've played with subs here and there. Everything was extremely short-term—nothing longer than a weekend here and there. I didn't trust my skills or judgment enough for anything more. I'm not that same man, though. I've grown in confidence and have faced the demons in my past.

"I'm a Dominant, Svetlana. I want to be *your* Dominant."

"If I decided to move forward with this." She holds up the contract. "Couples negotiating a contract shouldn't be sexually involved."

"That's true. If we'd just met, I'd insist on it." Lana narrows her eyes. "But we're already together. It doesn't make much sense for us to take a step backward. Unless you want to."

"I wouldn't agree to this if sex was off the table." She gives me a cheeky smile.

"I do think we should put some rules into play, though."

I grab a pen, and we make a list of fair negotiating guidelines, including not using sex as a bargaining chip. We're still talking when Lana yawns. "You must be exhausted."

"I am."

"It's time for bed. We'll pick up where we left off tomorrow." I reach out to pick up her copy of the contract.

"Wait. I want to take a picture to send to Grayson."

I pull my hand back as though the papers are on fire. "Who the hell is Grayson?"

Svetlana

I DON'T REALIZE WHAT I'VE SAID UNTIL AFTER THE words are out. I wasn't purposely keeping Gray a secret. Well, maybe I was. Telling the guy you're dating that you're still going to therapy because you've not come to terms with your sister's abduction, rape, and murder is not the easiest thing to do. I've thought about it but could never find the right words, so I let it go.

"Grayson's my therapist. Star put me in touch with him."

"When?" Brandon asks through gritted teeth.

"I've been seeing him for a little over a year."

"Why are you sending him a copy of the contract?"

"Gray's a kink-friendly therapist." I reach out and take Brandon's hand in mine. "He knows what happened between Slava and me and about you. I want to get his thoughts on the contract."

"Why didn't you tell me? Did you think it would change my feelings toward you?"

"I don't know. I guess I didn't realize." I stumble over my words. "I didn't think we were anything more than—"

"Fuck buddies? Wow." Brandon gets off the bed and walks to the other side of the room. "Now I feel like the fool."

"It's not like that." I get up and go to him. "I've been waiting for the other shoe to drop. For you to get sick of me. Like everyone else does," I say that last part quietly. Then, I walk around to stand in front of him. "I didn't think someone like you could care about someone like me. My negative self-thoughts are one of the things Gray and I have been working on."

"Svetlana, I could never see you as only someone to warm my bed until the next pretty thing comes along. Whether you consent to become my submissive or not, I need you to know that you're worth so much more than that."

Brandon's words burrow their way deep inside my heart, where I'm hoping they take root. "I'm learning."

"And if you let me, I want to be the one here every day to remind you."

"I'd like to negotiate the contract. If you're still okay with that. But I need to go slow."

"We can talk about that tomorrow. Right now." Brandon turns me around to face the bed. "You need to sleep."

I wake before Brandon and carefully slide out of bed to grab my phone. I quietly go downstairs to the kitchen to grab a coffee. After Alex took his collar off, I was certain that Brandon would offer me a contract, but he never did.

My first term at NYU is coming to a close. Natalie's packed and ready to return home for the Christmas holidays. Since we don't celebrate American Christmas, I decided to stay with Alex and see what the holiday is like here.

"Are you sure you don't want to come home with me?" Natalie asks. "I hate the idea of you staying here alone."

"I won't be alone. I'm going to stay at my friend's house."

*"The same mysterious friend you visit almost every weekend?"
she asks, her voice rising in pitch.*

"Yes."

"I'm convinced this friend is a secret boyfriend."

"I can assure you this is not a secret boyfriend," I smile.

*Several times, I have considered telling Natalie about Alex and
Brandon. Every time I go to open my mouth, I stop myself. Even
though we're roommates and have become fast friends, Natalie
knows relatively little about my personal life. She was raised to not
ask questions about things she isn't directly involved in, and even
then, she doesn't pry. In this case, it's worked to my advantage. I
keep a lot hidden from most people. Secrets I don't want to talk
about. Things Natalie could never understand.*

*Living in New York has been everything I dreamed it would be.
It's my chance to be me, not the daughter of a mob boss. Not the girl
whose sister was trafficked and murdered. Not even the girl who's
involved in BDSM. Just plain Svetlana Solonik.*

*Natalie's phone chimes. "It's my ride." She surprises me by
throwing her arms around my neck. "I'm going to miss you."*

*"We'll see each other in a few weeks," I say, squeezing her back.
"Have a nice time at home."*

"I will." She grabs her rolling suitcase and strolls out the door.

*After she leaves, I grab my bag and head outside to find Pyotr,
who's just pulling up in the car with Viktor.*

Over the years, I convinced myself it was never going to
happen. I knew Brandon was holding something about his past
back. At one point, I asked Alex, hoping he'd tell me Brandon's
secrets, but being a good friend, he did not.

Waiting was a difficult thing for me to do, especially at first.
My initial reaction was to do something stupid and force Brandon
to tell me. Looking back, I'm so thankful I didn't do that. After I
started seeing Grayson, one of the things we worked on was giving
others space to tell their story if and when they were ready.

Last night, Brandon opened up to me about Celia and everything that happened that night, including the loss of their unborn child and how that affected him. It was a moment that brought us closer together.

While I sip the hot coffee, I check my texts to see if Gray replied to my text from last night.

Grayson: I got the pictures you sent. Before I comment, I'd like to get your thoughts.

Me: Brandon caught me off guard with the whole idea.

As much as I don't want to, I tell Gray everything that happened last night. It wasn't my finest moment, but I've learned telling him everything is important.

Grayson: Do we need to go over the importance of proper vetting?

Me: No. He and I have already talked about it.

Grayson: I can already hear it. *But...*

Me: You're very perceptive.

Grayson: That's what I'm told. Now spill it.

Me: But this isn't a typical scenario. We've been together for a long time and already know so much about each other.

Grayson: That's true. However, this represents a considerable shift in your relationship—in the dynamics of it. Not taking your time here or skipping this step entirely could cause problems in the future.

Since when is Gray so gloom and doom? I don't see the point in vetting. We've already done that without putting a label on it. And I'm sure there won't be a long and drawn-out negotiation. Sure, we need to discuss limits, but beyond that, I don't see much else.

Me: I'll take that into consideration.

Grayson: Since I'm already on the subject of things you don't want to hear. I'm also going to urge you to take a step back on your physical relationship through this stage.

Me: Probably not

Grayson: Lana...

Me: Gray...

Brandon appears in the doorway wearing only his pajama pants.

"Why didn't you wake me?"

"You never sleep in. I figured you needed the rest."

"Who are you talking to?"

"Grayson."

Brandon doesn't respond. The subject of Grayson will take a bit more hashing out. While I wrap things up with Gray, Brandon grabs a mug and makes himself a coffee.

Me: I have to go.

Grayson: Please think about what I said.

"What's on your agenda today?" I ask as Brandon sits across from me.

"Negotiations," he says with a smile. "If you're okay with that."

After breakfast and a quick shower, we sit across from each other at the dining table. The first part of the contract outlines any medical issues we need to be aware of. Next, we discuss safewords. We've already been using red, green, and yellow, so we decide to keep those. Brandon also suggests adding hand signals if we do a scene where I'm gagged.

"Let's talk about triggers," Brandon says, moving to the next section. "In your previous experiences, has anything come up?"

"Not really."

Brandon leans forward on his elbows. "This section is important. Not that the others aren't. We've both experienced traumas. I want to be sure we don't rush through this and overlook anything."

"I agree. Maybe it's because I haven't had any long-term dynamics, but I haven't run into anything triggering."

"Nothing that happened with Slava that you feel should be addressed in this section?"

I'm sure he's referring to my refusing to talk to Slava after our contract expired like I agreed to. I don't consider that a trigger so much as a mistake I've learned from and hope not to repeat.

"No, I don't think so."

Brandon watches me closely for a few seconds. "I'm okay to move on, but I'd like to revisit this topic before we sign anything."

Brandon

"What about this section?" Svetlana points to the paper. "What we'll call each other."

"I'm partial to *papillion*." I smile. "Is there anything you'd like to call me?"

"I like Master."

"No," I answer quickly. "Anything but that."

"Why?"

"That's what Celia called me. I think we just found my first trigger." I flip back a few pages and make a note of that.

"I'm sorry."

"It's okay. You didn't know. How about we go with Sir?"

"I can agree to that, Sir," Svetlana says, then bites her bottom lip. "What about when other people are around? People who aren't in the lifestyle?"

"I'm fine with you calling me Brandon in those scenarios," I say, turning the page. "Limits. This is another area that we'll start discussing today, but we'll leave it open for anything that comes up."

I've already listed some hard limits, things I already know are also limits for Lana. There will be no illegal activities, sexual or otherwise, no toilet play, infantilism, cutting, catheters, or guns.

"No fire play?" she asks. "Why not?"

"I have no experience with it."

"I've never done it either, but it's something I'd like to try. Can we move it to soft limits pending more education?"

"That's fair." I jot down a note to ask Owen and Star about education on fire play.

"Humiliation is a hard no for me," Lana adds. "One of the Doms I played with in Moscow was really into that. I agreed to it for a scene one night and had to safeword. I can take all sorts of physical pain. Actually, I quite like pain, but not from words. I can't handle that."

"I'll put that on the hard limit list."

We take our time reviewing a list of common and not-so-common things and assigning them to hard, soft, or acceptable limits. There's still a lot more to go through. "Why don't we stop here for today." We don't have to force the conversation into one afternoon. "Are you planning to stay here tonight?"

"I told Natalie I'd be home tonight. Is that okay?"

"It actually works out well. I'm supposed to go to the club with Alex, and I felt bad about leaving you here alone."

"What's going on at the club tonight?"

"There's a roundtable for the Dominants."

"I'm glad you brought up Dominants. I have to call Alex and make arrangements to get my things. I left it all at his house."

"Go call him while I clean this stuff up."

After I gather the papers, I go in search of Pyotr. He has a key to my house and let himself in last night after Lana's search for the invisible woman. I find him downstairs watching television.

The basement level of my home is its own apartment. When my parents were still alive, this is where I lived. It allowed me the freedom to come and go while being right here if my ailing parents needed anything.

I think Pyotr enjoys the downtime he gets when we're here. I don't think he's heard me come in, but he turns my way. "Everything okay?"

"Lana had to make a few phone calls. She's going back to her place this evening."

"I'll be here when she's ready."

"Great. I'll let her know." I turn to go back upstairs.

"Do you have a minute?" Pyotr asks.

"Sure. What's up?"

"You know I've known Lana since she was a little girl."

This sounds like it might get serious, so I sit on the other end of the couch. "Yes."

"I've been by her side when she was at her lowest. The past few years, I've witnessed a lot of personal growth in her," Pyotr says, clearly proud of her. "I know she can be a challenge at times. Lana does her very best to push people away before they have a chance to hurt her."

"It's understandable, given what she's experienced."

Pyotr nods. "She's made some questionable relationship choices in her past. I'm sure she's told you about Slava."

"She has."

"I didn't approve of him."

"Why not?" Lana hasn't told me anything about this. I'm curious to hear Pyotr's thoughts.

"Lana was barely twenty at the time, and Slava was in his mid-thirties. I'm still not sure why Max didn't kill him," Pyotr chuckles. "Ordinarily, I could care less about a person's age, but this situation was different," he explains. "Lana talked a good game, but in reality, she was very impressionable—naïve."

"I thought he treated her well."

"He didn't hurt her, but in my opinion, Slava didn't take the time to get to know her. If he did, he would've seen the little girl inside that was begging for attention. She clung to anything or, in his case, anyone seeking comfort. Those are not the right reasons to be in a relationship." Pyotr is tense as he speaks. Although he's never said anything out loud, I know he cares a great deal about Svetlana. "I don't know much about this BDSM stuff other than the relationships can be complex. Which is all the more reason to not enter one with someone who isn't on a level playing field."

"That's a very good observation."

"Slava did it anyway. Because of that, Lana was hurt. Slava was, too. He isn't my responsibility, and frankly, I was glad he was out of her life."

Listening to Pyotr's observations, I'm beginning to grow nervous. Is he trying to tell me he doesn't approve of my presence in her life? What will I do if that's what he says next? My fears are put to rest with his next statement.

"I'm glad you came along," he says. "You see beneath the mask Svetlana wears."

"Before I met Lana, I'd heard a lot about her from Maxim and Alex. The topic of conversation was always about how difficult she was. One evening, Alex invited me for dinner. I had a few minutes alone with Viktor, so I asked him what his thoughts were," I say. "Viktor told me there was more to her that most people miss. I didn't want that to be me, so instead of going into it with preconceived ideas, I chose to forget everything I was told. I paid attention to the young woman telling me all about living in a new country and her excitement about starting school."

I smile, remembering that night as though it were just yesterday. "Sure, I saw the strong-willed girl she wanted everyone to see. But it was when she didn't think anyone was watching that I saw it. A scared, vulnerable young woman with a soft heart—one that deserved to be treasured."

"I was waiting for you to find her," Pyotr says with an emotion I can only describe as love.

"What do you mean?"

"I don't have a family of my own. Svetlana's the closest thing I'll ever have to one. I've watched men come and go. The one thing they all had in common was none of them ever deserved the love she has to give." He pauses. "You're different, Carpenter. When you look at her, I have no doubt you see what's beneath her protective exterior. You very well might be the right man for her."

"I'm in love with her." Pytor's the only person, other than Lana, who knows the depth of my feelings for her.

Pyotr smiles approvingly, then the smile slips from his face. He puts his finger in my face. "Don't do anything to fuck it up."

"Got it."

"What time will she be ready to leave?" And just like that, the threatening bodyguard disappears, and the mood lightens.

It takes me a minute to get my thoughts together after Pyotr's warning. He's fiercely protective of Lana. At times, I thought that maybe he was interested in her romantically, but that couldn't be further from the truth. All this time, he's been waiting for someone deserving of her to come along. I'm honored he believes that man is me. I'll do everything in my power to live up to his expectations.

After I make arrangements for Lana's ride, I go in search of her. My bedroom door is open, and I hear the shower water running. Lana's curvy silhouette is visible through the steamy glass door. She hasn't heard me come in, and I use that to my advantage, watching her run her hands over her body while I remove my clothes.

I pull open the shower door and Lana shrieks. "You scared me," she says, trying to catch her breath.

"Were you expecting someone else?" I raise an eyebrow.

"You're so funny." She reaches to smack my chest, but I grab her wrist and spin her around.

"Put your hands on the wall and bend over," I instruct, and use my foot to spread her legs. Reaching around her to the shelf, I grab the lube and squirt a generous amount on my fingers, then slowly slide my fingers in, stretching her and readying her for my cock. "Every part of you belongs to me."

"Mhm."

"Tell me." I've never felt the need to hear that a woman is mine as strongly as I do with Lana.

"Every part of me belongs to you," Lana says, looking over her shoulder.

"Are you ready?"

"Yes."

I pull my fingers out and add more lube to my dick before lining it up at her entrance. I push the tip past the tight ring of muscle and pause. As much as I want to plow into her and take her rough against the wall, I don't. All it would do is hurt her and tear her body. I don't want that, so I wait for her body to relax and allow me inside.

Inch by slow inch, I push my way into her. Taking her ass feels different than anything else. It's tight, almost painfully so, but I'm addicted to having her this way. I love walking the fine line between pain and pleasure with her. "Are you ready?"

"Yes," Lana says, her voice low and breathy.

Slowly, I start moving. The sensation of being squeezed by her body is overwhelming, and I struggle to not finish quickly like an inexperienced schoolboy. I have to remain focused so this can last for as long as possible.

Hot water streams over my back as my hand tangles in her long brown hair, wrapping it around my hand. "I'm getting close, *papillion*. I want you there with me."

Lana's hand drops between her legs. "Can you do it harder, Sir?"

Her words cause my fraying self-control to snap. With my free hand, I grab her waist to steady her as I give her exactly what she asked for.

"Yes, just like that," she encourages me.

"Fuck, Lana," I growl. "Come with me, now."

Lana's body squeezes my cock. Every nerve ending in my body is on fire, and I come deep inside her.

"It's too much, Sir. I can't." Lana's legs begin to give out from the force of her orgasm. I wrap my arm around her, holding her up as we ride out the ecstasy of our orgasms together.

The sound of our breathing mixes with the falling water from the shower. Lana inhales sharply as I pull out of her. When I'm sure she can stand, I loosen my hold on her. She turns around to face me. "That was incredible."

"We're made for each other, *papillon*. I want forever with you."

"I'm not—."

I place my finger on her lips, stopping her. I'm aware that I asked for more time when Lana was ready for more. The tables have turned. I'm sure of what I want, but now it's Lana who's asking for more time. "What do I need to do?"

"Just keep being you."

Svetlana

NEGOTIATING A CONTRACT WITH BRANDON WAS supposed to be easy. It's what I'd been waiting for since we first met. So, why, now that it's happening, am I having second thoughts and dragging my feet? It's been one month, and I'm still unable to sign and make the commitment.

While Brandon finishes his shower, I make breakfast. Whenever I stay at his house, which is more and more often, I cook the meals. It's a simple domestic thing to do that usually brings me great pleasure, but today, it's making my heart pound and hands tremble.

"You look tense," Brandon says, coming up behind me and wrapping his arms around my waist. "Is everything okay?"

"I'm a bit preoccupied thinking about an important paper due this week." I'm not ready to discuss the second thoughts I'm having yet. Mostly because I don't know what they are or why I feel this way. But I do know that I don't want to risk losing him.

"My office is at your disposal if you need the computer," he says as he sits at the table.

"I appreciate that, but everything I need is at my apartment," I say as I plate his French Toast. "I need to go home this afternoon so I can finish it up."

"Oh." The smile fades from his face. "I thought you'd spend the rest of the weekend."

"I really can't."

"That's okay. Maybe next time." The disappointment on his face is nearly my undoing. The words *I'll stay* are on the tip of my tongue, but they disappear with Brandon's next words. "When can I meet your roommate?"

I set our plates on the table and sit across from him before answering, "I don't know."

Natalie and I have gotten to be good friends, best friends, I'd like to say. But at the same time, I'm hiding a whole part of my life from her. I hate doing this, especially when she's been so open with me about everything in her life. This is different, though. I'm sure Natalie's never heard of the BDSM lifestyle, let alone was ever friends with someone involved in it. She clings to her conservative upbringing like it's a lifeline. Without it, she'll drown. The times I've suggested taking even a small step away from it and embracing different ideas, she's nearly shut down.

"She really doesn't know anything about your father or the lifestyle?" Brandon asks as he eats.

"Nothing. Natalie believes Papa's involved in the natural gas industry in Russia. She has no idea about his connections with the Bratva. And she definitely doesn't know anything about BDSM."

"Wow. It's hard to imagine being an adult with such a sheltered view of life."

"Natalie's lived a very sheltered life. Even though she's away for school, she's still very controlled by her parents and her boyfriend."

"Hopefully, you find a way because I'd really like to be a part of your life outside our little bubble."

Brandon's words have played on repeat in my head all afternoon. Even as Pyotr drops me off this evening, I can't stop thinking about it. I'd love to have him meet Natalie. To have him come to my apartment like a *regular* boyfriend, but I don't see how that could ever be possible.

When I get inside, Natalie's sitting on the couch with her textbooks and notebooks scattered around her. She looks up when I walk into the room. "I didn't think you'd be home today."

"I have a big paper due, and I forgot to bring my stuff with me." I quickly change the subject.

"What smells so good?"

"I'm making lasagna. It's my grandma's recipe." She smiles proudly.

"I'm glad I came home early because it smells divine."

Natalie giggles. "I made enough to freeze, so we'll have a few dinners pre-made for another night."

"You're amazing." I flop onto the loveseat and rest my head back. "I think I might take a nap. I'm exhausted."

"What do you do at your *close family friend's house* that you come home exhausted all the time?"

"What?" My head pops up.

"You always come home and say you're exhausted. Then, you go for a nap." Natalie tilts her head. "Don't you get any sleep wherever it is you disappear to?"

"We go out a lot. You know, and stay out late. Things you should be doing." I elbow her playfully.

"Things I shouldn't be doing because I have a boyfriend."

"Having a boyfriend doesn't mean you can't go out and have fun. It's not like you're going to cheat on him. You're just setting your schoolwork aside and going out with your girlfriends for a few hours. It's okay to take a break and have fun every now and then."

Natalie closes her tablet in her textbooks and quickly gathers her things. "I'm going to go to my room to study. I have an exam on Monday."

"I'm sorry, Nat. I didn't mean—"

"It's fine, really. I have a lot of schoolwork I need to get done," she says as she hurries out of the room.

I drop my head back again and groan. This is precisely why I try not to bring these things up. If Natalie and I can't even talk about these things, how could I ever initiate a conversation about the more taboo parts of my life? I don't see any possible way for her to meet Alex and Brandon.

Svetlana

"You don't have to drive me to the airport. I can take an Uber," Natalie says for the millionth time.

"It's not a problem. Pyotr doesn't mind." I was forced to tell Natalie about Pyotr a few months after we started rooming together.

Natalie and I were coming home from a TED Talk the school hosted. It was late, so we cut through Washington Square Park on the way back to our dorm when we were approached by a group of drunk guys who were coming back from a frat party. Pyotr allowed me the space to deal with them on my own, but when they wouldn't take no for an answer and were starting to get handsy with us, he stepped out of the shadows.

I still laugh when I think about the looks on their faces when my well-built and intimidating Russian bodyguard educated them on proper behavior around women. When he was through with his lesson, Pyotr forced them to apologize to us, which I don't think any of those guys had ever done. They thought they were off the hook, and then Pyotr issued a very up close and personal threat that had them shaking in their skin as they scurried away.

Of course, after that, I had to tell Natalie about Pyotr. It's a tried-and-true story based on truth that I've used for years. Papa's work in the natural gas industry has made him a great deal of money. With that also comes many enemies. Because of that, he insists I always have security with me. Natalie didn't question that rationale at all. She was just happy Pyotr was there to help us out.

Since then, Pyotr has been able to have a little more of an open presence in my life, which makes Papa and him happy. We even had him over for dinner a few times.

"Are you sure you don't want to come with me?" Natalie asks. "I hate knowing you're going to be alone for Thanksgiving."

"I've never celebrated Thanksgiving, so I'm not missing anything," I say, smiling. "I promise I'll be fine." I'll be more than fine. I have some very hot plans with a certain man I know.

"If we don't leave now, you'll miss your flight," Pyotr calls from the kitchen.

"We're coming." Natalie and I grab her luggage and hurry down the hall.

"I'll get those." Pyotr takes the bags from us, and we go outside to the car.

"I hate this," Natalie complains as we sit at a dead stop on the highway. "That's one nice thing about Northmeadow. There's never any traffic."

"No, but we have gotten stopped by cows standing in the middle of the road." We both laugh. "Honestly, I don't know how you go back to that after being here with all this."

"New York is only temporary. Northmeadow is home."

"I guess." I shrug. "I could never live in such a small town."

"It'd be different if you knew your future was there." Natalie smiles. "I have a job waiting for me, and after Thanksgiving break, I'll have a fiancé there, too."

"I can't believe you're getting engaged." I try my best to sound happy for her.

"Tommy hasn't said it for sure, but he's been giving lots of big hints."

"Don't you think you're too young to get married?"

"Most of my girlfriends are already married. Some even have children."

I don't have to fake my reaction because I'm honestly shocked. "You're kidding?"

"No. I told you, girls from Northmeadow don't go to college. After high school, we're expected to marry and stay home to raise our children."

"Wanting to get married and have children are wonderful things. I'm not arguing that. But why is getting an education not valued?" I ask, genuinely confused. "What if you want to work?"

"Because of my scholarship, I'll be working for at least a few years."

Natalie's road to NYU was even more difficult than mine. Her desire to attend university was a foreign concept to her parents. In their eyes, Natalie was expected to graduate high school, marry Tommy, pop out his babies, and live the same life her parents had. When she approached them with her desire to attend college, they were furious and refused to help her.

Natalie thought her dreams were over until Ms. Campbell, the head of her local school district, approached her with an offer she couldn't refuse. This woman knew Natalie was still recovering from her brother, Michael, and his boyfriend Evan's suicide. Ms. Campbell wasn't originally from Northmeadow and held a different view of the world outside the small town. She also realized that there would be more tragedies if something wasn't done to address the needs of the young people in town.

Ms. Campbell, on behalf of the school board, offered Natalie a full scholarship for both undergrad and graduate school. It paid for everything down to her books with the caveat that she returned to Northmeadow and remain employed by the school district for five years.

When Natalie first told me the terms of the scholarship, I was shocked. Signing up for a five-year employment commitment sounded insane to me. Natalie earned her bachelor's degree with a 4.0 GPA. She's already receiving job offers from agencies in the city, but she's had to turn them all down because of her restrictive scholarship.

I understand why she accepted it, though. Without it, she would've had no way to go to school, and that was something she couldn't live with. Making this move was the only act of rebellion she's ever done. I'm surprised her mother didn't lock Natalie in her room until she saw *reason,* according to them.

"I'm glad about that. You deserve to do what you want with your life before and even after becoming a mom."

"Tommy's everything I want in life," she says dreamily. "I'm going to have the best life ever."

"I'm so excited for you." As much as I want to shake some sense into her, Natalie's going home to get engaged. Now's not the time to argue with her. If she's truly happy with the path she's on, then I'll be here cheering her on every step of the way. "You better send me pictures of your ring."

The JFK airport is like a city inside the city. Roads twist and turn, leading in so many directions. I'm thankful I don't have to figure out where we're going because we'd never get there. Pyotr doesn't have an issue navigating through the maze, bringing us to where we need to go with apparent ease.

He pulls into a parking spot and starts getting out of the car.

"You guys don't have to walk me in," Natalie says. "I'm sure you have better things to do."

"Don't be silly. I have nothing better to do," I say, linking my arm with hers. "I added some stuff to your wedding board on Pinterest."

"Thank you. I'll look at it after I'm home." We get to the terminal, and Natalie stops walking. Turning to me, she says, "I know you think I'm crazy for getting engaged so young, and it's no secret you aren't Tommy's biggest fan. Which makes me even more grateful for your support."

"I'll always be in your corner."

"Will you be my maid of honor?" Natalie asks.

"Of course," I squeal and wrap Natalie in a tight hug. "I love you, girly."

"Love you too, Lan."

"Have fun, and text me as soon as you're officially an engaged woman."

"I will."

"Have a safe flight," Pyotr adds.

"Thanks for the ride." Natalie stands on her toes and surprises Pyotr by kissing his cheek before she takes her bag.

We watch as she goes through the security checkpoint. She gives us a small wave before disappearing into the waiting area to board her flight.

"You did good, little butterfly," Pyotr says as we return to the car.

"What do you mean?"

"Her soon-to-be-fiancé is a prick, but for some reason, she loves him. I'm proud of you for being supportive rather than arguing with her."

"I've tried arguing. It doesn't work." I shrug. "All I can do is be her friend."

"Natalie's a genuinely sweet girl," Pyotr says with a smile. "She deserves so much better."

"I couldn't agree with you more."

When we first left for the airport, I texted Brandon.

Me: We're leaving now. I'll see you soon.

Brandon: I'll be waiting.

I knew Natalie would be out of town for the week, so I gave Brandon a set of keys to the apartment. Although I still haven't agreed to sign the contract, we're doing what I'm sure will be a hot scene. Brandon was apprehensive about doing a consensual, non-consensual role-play, but I really wanted to try it. It took a lot of negotiation and safeguards before he agreed.

My job was to let him know what we were leaving for the airport. After that, we won't have any more contact until the scene starts. We didn't put an exact time on when we're starting. Not knowing when it'll happen should keep the scene as authentic as possible.

The drive home doesn't take as long as it did to get to the airport. Pyotr pulls to a stop outside my apartment. "Do you want company, little butterfly?"

"No thanks. I'm going to get some studying done."

"You are going to use your break to study?" Pyotr raises an eyebrow. "Where are you really planning on going?"

"You can relax." I step out of the car. "I'm not going anywhere."

"You're up to no good."

"I'll call you if I need you." I close the door and wave goodbye.

Pyotr watches as I walk up to the door. Goosebumps run up and down my spine, and I get the feeling I'm being watched.

That's probably because I am.

Brandon

When Lana asked me about a CNC scene, my first instinct was to run screaming in the other direction. It brought up too many memories of that awful night with Celia. I didn't want to involve Alex, but I had to talk to someone about it.

He reminded me that what Lana and I are doing is consensual. What happened to Celia was non-consensual, and they are two very different things. Lana and I planned out everything that would happen tonight, including the element of surprise.

The other part of my hesitation is due to Lana's past. As a little girl, she experienced her sister being abducted from right next to her. She wasn't there to witness anything and still doesn't know the details. But given the circumstances, it's safe to say Jelena was raped and tortured. Even though this scene was her idea, I've been struggling with the possibility of doing something that will unknowingly trigger her.

I was less than thrilled when Lana told me she consulted her therapist, Grayson, about our scene. My jealous, irrational side doesn't want her confiding in another man about what we do together. Alex was the voice of reason that forced me to step back and try to look at things through her eyes. He also suggested the possibility of going to an appointment with her. It wasn't until I attended my first session that I became comfortable with the situation. Grayson is completely professional and has Lana's best interests at heart.

Since then, Lana and I have gone to several sessions together to discuss tonight's scene in more detail. It's been helpful for me to learn what to do if something triggers Lana. We talked about body cues Lana often gives before she's consciously aware that something's about to affect her. Those sessions, along with having safe words and signals built into every part of tonight, have given me the confidence to move forward.

While Lana was out, I went into her apartment to set up a few things, including two small wireless cameras to watch her movements. As soon as Svetlana gets home, there's no doubt she'll know someone's been in there.

I'm just getting home when I get a text.

Pyotr: Lana's up to something.

Me: What do you mean?

Pyotr: I just dropped her off and offered to keep her company, but she told me she's going to study. It's a school holiday. I KNOW she's not studying.

I'm trying to formulate a response when I get another text.

Pyotr: Maybe I should hang around, just in case.

Me: I don't think you need to do that.

Actually, that's the last thing I want.

Pyotr: What do you know that I don't?

Me: I'm going to her place tonight. I'll make sure she stays out of trouble.

Pyotr: Why didn't she tell me you were coming over? I don't have to worry about her if you're there.

Me: I'm sure she was embarrassed. Thanks for the heads up, though. I appreciate it.

Pyotr: Have a good night.

Now, I wait until I'm ready to make my next move.

Svetlana

WITH EACH STEP I TAKE, I CAN'T HELP BUT LOOK OVER my shoulder. I know it's just Brandon stalking me, but that doesn't stop the anxiety I'm experiencing. As soon as I'm in my apartment, I lock the door behind me. Not that it will do much. He has a key.

As I walk through the living room, something on the fireplace mantle catches my eye. One of our picture frames is turned backward. I know it wasn't that way when I left. With cautious steps, I make my way across the room and right the frame. When I step into the kitchen, I find a vase with a red rose in the middle of the island. That wasn't there when I left. Is Brandon already here?

On the way to my room, I open the doors to the guest bathroom, extra bedroom, and Natalie's bedroom checking each one before closing the door and going to my room. My hand trembles as I turn the handle and push the door open. After a thorough search, I'm confident I'm still alone, but for how long?

Brandon

THE CAMERAS I PLACED ALLOW ME TO WATCH LANA AS she finds the things I left behind. She knows I've been in her apartment. She's on high alert right now, so I'm sitting back and biding my time. I don't plan to make another move until Lana's relaxed and lets her guard down.

It's late. Lana's beyond pacing and looking out the windows. She gave up on that hours ago. That's when I went back into the city to grab some dinner. After I ate, I came to Washington Square Park, where I've been enjoying a quiet evening of people-watching.

Lana has just finished watching a movie and is walking to her bedroom. I watch as she strips her clothes and walks into her bathroom for what I'm assuming is a shower. That's when I decide to make my move.

Once inside the apartment, I lock the door and quietly walk down the hall to her bedroom. The shower water's still running, so I hurry to set up a few things before she comes out. Then, I sit on the edge of her bed and wait.

The water shuts off, and my heart rate increases, knowing when Lana opens the door, I'm the first thing she'll see, and our scene will start. My intent is to catch her off guard and startle her. It's all part of the scene. It's also a fine line between CNC and true fear—a line I don't intend to cross.

The handle on the bathroom door turns, and Lana steps across the threshold. She's looking down at her phone as she pulls the door closed. Everything begins moving in slow motion as her blue eyes meet mine. She gasps and drops her phone. I stand and close the gap between us, caging her against the door with my arms.

"Do not make a sound." I keep my voice low. "Nod your head if you understand."

Her head lifts and lowers slowly.

Reaching out, I tug on the towel wrapped around her and watch it fall to the floor, puddling at her feet. Goosebumps cover her still-damp skin. I reach out and squeeze one of her already hard nipples. "I'm going to have fun with this hot little body tonight." I grab her arm and try to drag her to the bed.

"No, please. Don't hurt me," she cries. "I have money. I can get you as much as you want."

"I didn't come here for money. Be a good girl, and don't cause a scene." I tug harder, encouraging her to move. Lana stumbles into me. My hard cock presses against her toned abdomen. She inhales sharply, and I know she feels it. "You want some of this?" I thrust against her.

"No," she spits.

"Don't play hard to get, sweetheart."

"Let me go. If my bodyguard comes back here, he'll—"

"You sent him away hours ago." I move closer to her face. "Now listen to me closely. You need to close those pretty lips unless you want to find them wrapped around my cock." Her mouth snaps shut. "Now, get over here."

I drag her across the room and push her onto her bed. Lana fights hard, so I straddle her body to gain control. Taking her left arm, I pull it over her head. A loud click sounds as I snap the cuff around her wrist. "No. Please let me go." I ignore her plea and cuff her other arm above her head. Then, I move to her legs. Lana doesn't make it easy. She fights me at every turn.

The fear I see in her eyes and hear in her voice feels too real. It takes all my self-control to stay in character—to remind myself this is all planned. Lana agreed to be fully restrained. We planned that she'd beg me to stop. That she'd fight back, and I'd ignore it. Other than the warning signs Grayson and I reviewed, this scene stops only if she says yellow or red.

Once her legs are secure, I step back. Lana's naked body is spread out. Every inch is on display for me, and she's bound to the bed. Her dark hair, still wet from her shower, fans out messily around her. She's never looked more beautiful than she does right now—completely powerless and at my mercy.

Rather than terrifying me, the knowledge that I'm solely responsible for her safety while she surrenders control turns me on. My dick strains inside my jeans.

"We're going to have so much fun tonight," I say and drag my finger through her wet pussy. She's enjoying this as much as I am.

"I don't want any of this."

"Your body tells another story, sweetheart."

"Go to hell," she snarls.

I pull my T-shirt off and toss it onto the floor. "I warned you what would happen if you didn't keep your mouth shut." Reaching into my bag, I pull out the open-mouth gag I brought and dangle it in front of Svetlana. "This is my insurance policy. I don't want you getting any ideas about using those teeth while I fuck your face."

"No, please," she whimpers. "I promise I'll be quiet."

"It's too late for that," I chuckle.

I lean over her to fit the gag around her head. Lana thrashes her head back and forth, causing me to struggle with the latch.

"Hold your fucking head still," I say as the bedroom door flies open, banging off the wall, and a flashlight shines in our direction.

"Stop," a female voice yells. "The police are on their way."

"Natalie?" Lana shrieks as she lifts her head. "What are you doing here?"

Natalie? As in Natalie, her roommate, who has no idea that Lana's involved in the BDSM lifestyle or that she's dating me and has now walked in on a CNC scene. This isn't going to end well.

The ceiling light flips on. Natalie takes one look at Svetlana, splayed out and restrained on the bed, and she screams. Then, her focus shifts to me. "You. Don't move," she yells and points her phone at me. I drop the metal gag. It lands with a thud on the floor, and I put my hands up.

"Nat, this isn't what it looks like. Can you uncuff me?" Lana asks.

I look at Natalie and then back to Lana before quickly releasing her arms and legs.

"I thought you were in Missouri," Lana says as she jumps out of bed and grabs her robe. She ties the belt around her waist and hurries over to Natalie. "What are you doing home?"

"Are you okay?" She grabs Lana's arms and looks her up and down. "Did he hurt you?" Natalie asks and glares at me over Lana's shoulder.

Banging on the apartment door startles me. "NYPD, open up."

"Oh my God, you really called the police." Lana's voice is panicked.

"Of course, I called them."

There's pounding again. "NYPD, open the door."

"Come with me." Lana grabs Natalie's arm and drags her along. "We need to fix this."

Keeping a safe distance, I follow the girls out of the bedroom.

Lana heads straight to the door and unlocks it. "Good evening, officers. Please come in," she says calmly and steps aside, allowing them room to enter the apartment.

"We received a call of an assault in progress." The taller of the two male officers says.

I move to take a step closer when the other officer reaches for his gun. "You, put your hands up and don't move."

I freeze in place with my hands in the air.

Svetlana

"There's a very good explanation for all this," I say, hoping to find the right words to get us out of this mess without Brandon ending up in handcuffs. "Please put your weapons away." The police officer looks between Brandon and me. "That's my boyfriend. May I call him over?"

He doesn't take his hand off his weapon but says, "Yes."

I look behind me and see a confused Natalie sitting on the couch with her head in her hands. I'll take care of this with her later. Right now, I need to address the situation with law enforcement. I motion for Brandon to come over. He looks at me hesitantly before walking across the room.

"Officer, this is my boyfriend, Brandon Carpenter. My roommate was supposed to be out of town this week, so he and I planned some private couple's time."

"We got a call of an assault in progress," the office says.

"Brandon and I have very particular tastes when it pertains to intimate things." The officer looks between his partner and me. "We practice bondage and other more adventurous bedroom pursuits."

"I see." The man finally removes his hand from his weapon, replacing it into his holster.

"Natalie comes from a small mid-western town." I look over my shoulder at my roommate before continuing. "She's very sheltered and naïve. I haven't even told her I have a boyfriend."

"She was supposed to be gone home for the school holiday," Brandon adds. "We didn't expect her to walk in on us."

The officers separate Brandon and me and ask us more questions in their attempt to clarify what was going on and to be sure there was no crime in progress. It takes a bit of doing, but we finally convince them there was no wrongdoing.

"Thank you, and sorry for the confusion," I say, shaking the officers' hands before they leave the apartment. Then, I close the door and blow out a breath.

"Do you want me to stay?" Brandon asks, taking my hand in his. "I can help you explain."

"I don't think that's a good idea. I'll call you in the morning."

"Okay, talk to you tomorrow," he says, kissing my forehead before leaving.

I take my time locking up, knowing the conversation Natalie and I are about to have will be equally as difficult as dealing with the NYPD. After taking a deep breath, I turn on the lamp and sit beside Natalie on the couch. "I don't know where to start," I say and then turn to look at her. What I see concerns me. "You've been crying." She nods. "What's wrong? Why are you home?"

"Tommy," Natalie says, quickly changing the subject. "What was going on back there?"

I look down the hall toward my room before answering. "It wasn't what it looked like."

"Did he hurt you?"

"No. Well, not any more than I asked for." I can't help the giggle that slips out.

"What?" Natalie's clearly confused.

"I'm going to grab us a glass of wine. I think we're going to need it." I get up and go into the kitchen. While I get the glasses and open the bottle, I ask, "What happened with Tommy?"

"I got to his dorm and found him having sex with Ashlynn."

Holy shit. Forget about a glass. We may need the whole bottle. "Ashlynn, as in your best friend?" I ask as I hand Natalie her glass.

"The one and only."

"Wow."

"Right now, I'm more concerned about what was happening here," Natalie says, motioning around the room.

"I wasn't expecting you to be home." I take a sip of the red wine and then set my glass on the table. "What you saw wasn't what you thought. I mean, it was, but not like you think."

"You were handcuffed to the bed and begging him to stop. It looked like he was hurting you."

"Oh boy, I don't know where to start."

"How about the beginning?"

I don't think there's any way to do this, so I blurt out the question. "Have you ever heard of BDSM?"

Natalie nearly chokes on her wine. "I've read about it in some romance novels. It's all that kinky sex and stuff." Realization washes over her face the second the words are out. "Is that what was going on back there?" Her hands tremble as she sets her glass down.

"Yes," I say and slowly nod. "I grew up in the BDSM lifestyle. Papa's a Dominant, and Mama's his submissive."

Natalie's mouth hangs open. "You mean to tell me your dad goes all Christian Grey and ties your mom up in the bedroom?"

"Ha, ha. You're so funny." I can't help but laugh. "That's not exactly how it is in real life. My papa adores Mama, and she him. Their relationship has always been an example of what I hope to find someday."

Whenever I talk about my parent's relationship, I can't help but be filled with great pride. I've always loved watching the affection they showered on one another in words or actions. I never hid my eyes or pretended it was gross seeing Papa give Mama a chaste kiss or hug.

When I was young, I'd tug on Papa's leg, begging for my own kiss. He'd scoop me up and swing me around before placing a kiss on my cheek. As I grew older, I recognized the adoration in Papa's eyes when he'd quietly watch Mama demonstrate her love and respect for him through her actions. Whether or not I entered the lifestyle, I knew from a young age that I wanted to find a man who looked at me and loved me the way Papa does Mama.

"Why would you want to know what your parents get up to in their bedroom?" Natalie scrunches up her nose.

"Eww." I nearly vomit at the thought. "We didn't talk about any of that stuff. BDSM is about so much more than kinky sex."

Keeping Natalie's upbringing in mind, I explain that the kinky things in the bedroom are just the basics of everything BDSM encompasses. It's a lifestyle choice where the submissive, be they man or woman, cares for the daily wants and needs of their Dominant. The person willingly hands control of their life to another, trusting that person sometimes with their very life.

In return for their gift of submission, the Dominant challenges their submissive to grow, not only in their submission but as a person. They are the granters of pleasure and the administers of discipline. Dominants ensure their submissive is safe and cared for. More than that, they're adored and cherished by their Dominant.

"What you walked in on tonight." I pause, trying to find the right words. "That was a scene Brandon and I'd been planning for a while. You were supposed to be gone."

"Wait a minute. You do this BDSM thing, too?"

"I'm a submissive," I say without hesitation.

"How were we roommates for two years, and I never knew?" She turns to face me and sits cross-legged on the couch.

"It's not a topic that's easy to bring up. Hi," I say and extend my hand for a simulated greeting. "I'm your new dorm mate. I like to get tied up and whipped." We both laugh.

Part of the reason I kept this from Natalie was because I didn't know how to introduce someone who's had so few experiences to BDSM. It was easy for me. I've known about the lifestyle for as long as I can remember. My parents and I have a very open relationship. They didn't hide their involvement in the lifestyle, but they also didn't go into detail about their private sex life. I mean, why would they? Instead, they modeled a healthy Dominant/submissive relationship. Which really models a healthy, traditional husband and wife relationship.

"When I was about eighteen, I asked my parents more about the lifestyle," I explain. "We had many conversations where my parents emphasized the commitment required for this kind of relationship. From the beginning, I knew I was a submissive. Mama wasn't as easily convinced. She stressed the importance of being mature enough to put my needs second to someone else's. I know from experience it isn't as easy as it sounds."

I give Natalie a minute to digest what I said while I take a drink.

"Mama gave me some books to read and introduced me to a trusted friend who was an experienced submissive. I mentored under her until I went to Moscow to study. That's where I submitted to a Dominant for the first time."

"Do you still happen to have the books she gave you?" she asks, trying to sound nonchalant.

Natalie's question catches me off guard. "Why?"

"I figure reading them might come in handy when I graduate." She shrugs, feigning innocence.

"I've been to Northmeadow." I sit back and cross my arms. "I don't think your teen clients will be into BDSM."

"Maybe I'm curious."

The way she places emphasis on *I'm* makes my head spin. Never in a million years did I think that would be Natalie's reaction. "I'll be right back." If she wants to broaden her horizons and learn about something new, I won't stop her. I think it will be good for her to realize there's more to life than marrying young and having babies. I grab the e-reader from my bedroom and return to the living room. "They're loaded on here." I pass the tablet to her and return to sit. "Your turn. Tell me exactly what happened when you got to Mizzou."

"I was so excited to surprise Tommy." A stray tear trickles down her cheek. "But when the door to his dorm opened, and I saw them together, my perfectly constructed life fell apart. I've never felt so betrayed. That was my boyfriend and best friend." Natalie presses the heel of her palms against her eyes as she tries to stop the tears from falling. "Maybe my parents were right when they said I shouldn't leave town for school?"

I listen quietly, all the while seething inside. What kind of a person betrays their best friend like that? And Tommy, I'd love to see him alone in a room with Pyotr for a few minutes.

"Now I have to come up with an excuse to tell my parents," she says and yawns. "There's no way I'm going back there until I have to."

I grab our empty wine glasses and bring them to the kitchen. "Why don't you sleep on it first. We can come up with something later."

The sun's beginning to break through the dark night sky, and we're still awake. I know I'm tired, and Natalie must be past exhausted with everything she's been through tonight.

"You have to promise to tell me more about you being tied up by that hot guy." She smiles.

"I just hope he's still interested. Someone scared the shit out of him by calling the police." I link my arm through Natalie's as we walk to our rooms.

Natalie's room is before mine. "Thank you." She hugs me. "And I'm sorry I ruined your night."

"There's nothing to apologize for." I wipe a tear that drips down her cheek. "That's the last time you're allowed to cry over Tommy. You're far too good for him."

"Lana—"

"Don't Lana me. Tommy's a piece of shit, and I won't let you make excuses for him anymore," I say in my best bossy voice. "Tomorrow starts a whole new adventure. One where you get to determine your future."

"I love you."

"Love you more. Now get some sleep."

When I get to my room, I look around at the remnants of our interrupted scene. I'm disappointed that we didn't get to finish. Heck, we barely got started. Brandon left a key on the bedside table and use it to remove the cuffs from the bed. I pick up the gag from the floor and put it all in his bag.

After changing into soft pajamas, I grab my cell and climb into bed. I intend to text Brandon, but a wave of exhaustion washes over me, and I drift off to sleep before I hit send.

Brandon

LAST NIGHT WAS INSANE. WHEN I LEFT LANA'S, I WENT right home. But today, I need someone to help me process everything, so I shoot a text to Alex.

Me: Tell me you're not in the office.

Alex: I'm not in the office.

Me: Is that the truth, or are you just telling me what I want to hear?

Alex: I just got back from my run. How did everything go last night?

Me: I don't want to talk about it over text. Are you able to get together for lunch?

Alex: Sure. The regular place?

Me: Yeah. I'll meet you there in about an hour.

After a quick shower, I take the subway across town and walk the few blocks to the little bar. It's mid-afternoon, so the place is pretty quiet. I easily spot Alex in our usual booth in the back corner.

"You look awful," Alex smirks. "Must have been a pretty long night."

"You don't know the half of it." Our server comes to our

table, and we place our orders. Once he's gone, I say, "Things were just starting to heat up when her roommate showed up."

"You're kidding, right?"

I shake my head. "I wish I was. You think I can make this shit up? I couldn't have written that if I tried." I rewind and give Alex a brief outline of the events leading up to the bedroom door flying open. "Another few seconds and, well, things would've been even more uncomfortable. As it was, while Lana was trying to figure out why Natalie came home early, the NYPD started banging on the door."

Alex bursts out laughing. "I wish I was there to see you two trying to talk your way out of that one."

"It's not funny."

"You're right. It's hysterical."

"You wouldn't be laughing if you were the one with your hands in the air and a policeman pointing his weapon at you."

"Damn. They took it seriously."

"They received a phone call about an assault in progress. You're fucking right they took it seriously."

"I'm glad no one got hurt," Alex says, no longer laughing. "Now what?"

"I offered to stay and help Lana explain what happened to Natalie, but she wanted to do it herself."

"From what I've heard about that girl, that's probably a good idea." We stop talking while our food is served. "How are things there today?"

"I don't know. Lana hasn't called. I'm assuming she has a lot of explaining to do with her roommate, and I don't want to interfere."

"You also don't want her assuming you're mad or worse," Alex says.

He has a point. I need her to know we're still good. That last night's demise didn't scare me away. So, I pull out my phone.

Me: How was Natalie after I left? Is everything okay?

Lana: It went better than expected.

Me: Good. Can I come over today and officially meet your roommate?

Lana: I don't think that's a good idea. Natalie's been extra quiet. She came home early because she caught Tommy in bed with her best friend. Then everything with us. I think she's still trying to process everything.

Me: Maybe it'll help if we're both there to answer her questions.

Lana: I appreciate the offer, but I don't think that's a good idea. I want to keep everything calm and quiet today. I'll call you in a few days, okay?

Me: Okay.

I set the phone on the table and rub my hands over my head.

"What's wrong?"

"She doesn't want me to come over. That she'll call me in a few days." My heart sinks.

"Don't freak out yet. I'm sure she's overwhelmed with everything that happened last night. You know Lana, she retreats inward while she works things through."

"I'm sure you're right." Alex starts laughing again. "What?" I ask, slightly annoyed at his inappropriate response.

"I can't believe her roommate called the cops on you."

As hard as I try not to laugh, I lose the battle and join him.

Svetlana

NATALIE'S BEEN QUIET AND SPENDING MOST OF HER time in her room. I've been walking on eggshells, unsure of what to do. I know she's still heartbroken over what happened with her now ex-boyfriend. Add to that the shock of what she found the night she came home. It's a lot for anyone. At some point, she needs to talk about it—all of it. I'm just not sure how to bring any of it up.

I'm in the kitchen cooking when Natalie walks into the room. Without saying anything, she sits at the kitchen island, tapping her fingers on the granite counter.

I ignore the noise as long as I can before I spin around, spatula in hand. "You're driving me crazy with the nervous tapping. What's up?"

Her hand stills, but she doesn't speak for several long seconds. "I was wondering if I could ask you some more questions? You know, about the books I'm reading."

"Sure," I answer and turn back to the stove so my food doesn't burn.

"What're you making?" Natalie asks.

"Piroshki. It's kind of my mama's recipe, except I cheated and bought the dough," I say and smile. "But I don't think that's what you wanted to ask. Dinner's ready. We can eat and talk."

I set the table while Natalie pours the wine. With our plates full, I watch as she takes her first bite. "Oh my God, Lana. This is amazing," she says, closing her eyes.

"Thanks, but you're avoiding," I say, pointing my fork at her.

"I want to learn more," Natalie says quickly and then takes a bite.

I can't help but laugh. "That's what you were so nervous to say?"

She shrugs.

I swipe Natalie's phone and unlock the screen. Knowing each other's passwords comes in handy. "Here's the club I go to. It's called Fire and Ice." I pass the phone back to her so she can see the website. "They have classes for people who think they might be interested. You should take one."

"I'm not ready for anything like that," Natalie says, setting aside her phone. "Isn't there anything else I can read?"

"There are tons of books, but you'll learn more by taking the class and talking to real people."

"I'll think about it."

After we clean up, we settle on the couch with a bowl of popcorn. We've been watching popular American '80s movies. Tonight's flick is *The Breakfast Club*. I'm told it's a must-watch, and by the time the end credits roll, I totally understand why this movie is so loved. I didn't have to grow up in America to connect with the onscreen teenage struggles. They seem to transcend the boundaries of where a person is raised.

"Are you going to stay at your friend's house this weekend?" Natalie asks.

"I was thinking about it. Why? What's up?"

"I have Saturday off, and I was hoping to go shopping. I'm in need of a new wardrobe."

That's an offer I can't pass up. "I'll be ready bright and early."

"Thanks, Lana." Natalie smiles. "If we have a long day of shopping, I better get to sleep."

I haven't seen Natalie smile this much since she got back from her devastating trip home. Things were so bad after that she had to change her cell phone number because Tommy wouldn't stop harassing her. He obviously doesn't take hints very well.

She gave her parents her new number. As we figured, they haven't stopped bugging her about going home. She keeps giving them excuses about why she can't leave the city. I was afraid she'd cave and give in to their demands, but it seems like Natalie might be turning a corner with her independence.

I knew it was a big stretch asking Natalie to go to a club the other night, but I'd love for her to take the beginner class. It would put her in an environment with people who'll encourage her to stand up for herself and remind her that she has a voice in her life. For the first time in her life, she'd also be shown how she deserves to be treated by a man.

Since I don't think I can get her there, I'll have to talk to Gray and see if he has any other resources I can give Natalie. I don't want to push her too far out of her comfort zone. But if she wants to learn about the lifestyle and explore her developing sense of self, I plan to cheer her on.

Grayson

DECEMBER 11 SESSION NOTES

Today's the first time I've seen Svetlana since before the Thanksgiving holiday. She canceled her appointment last week because of illness.

The session started as per usual. Svetlana caught me up on the past several weeks, including the CNC scene she and Brandon did. Svetlana was not triggered in any way, which was a significant concern for her boyfriend. It was successful in many ways until her roommate, Natalie, unexpectedly showed up and called 911. According to Svetlana's account, she did a remarkable job handling the authorities and her traumatized roommate.

Of particular interest was the fact that she didn't mention anything about Brandon after that night. When I asked, she told me she texted him briefly the next day. He wanted to come over, and she refused. It appears she's kept him at arm's length ever since. She was not receptive to more questions about that subject, so I let it go. It is something I'm hoping to explore further in a future session.

After recapping recent events, I asked her what she wanted to discuss. Svetlana is always given the choice to lead the direction of our session.

Today, she was focused on her roommate, who has expressed curiosity about the BDSM lifestyle but is resistant to doing anything in person. Svetlana asked for more resources to give Natalie that would allow her to continue learning but in a more comfortable manner.

I provided Svetlana with several reputable websites to pass on to her roommate and an offer to speak with Natalie directly if she's interested.

My overall observations are that Svetlana remained guarded throughout today's session, preferring to shift the attention to Natalie rather than herself. Having worked with Svetlana for over a year, I know it's part of her pattern to have periods where she retreats. I've learned that where it may appear she's not making forward progress, she typically has a breakthrough in the weeks following a more reserved session.

Brandon

CHRISTMAS IS THIS WEEK. BEFORE THE CRAZINESS THAT happened over Thanksgiving break, Svetlana and I planned to spend the Christmas holiday together at her apartment. On Christmas Eve, we were to attend a Christmas party at Fire and Ice, where we were finally signing the contract, making our Dominant/submissive dynamic official. Afterward, we planned to drive to JFK, where Maxim's jet would be waiting to fly us to Russia to spend a few days with her family.

Everything changed after Natalie found her now ex-boyfriend with her now ex-best friend. Since then, Natalie refuses to go back to her hometown until she absolutely has to, which means she won't be out of town for the holiday. Svetlana's still not comfortable having Natalie and I interact. At first, I was upset and questioned if Svetlana was trying to push me away. When I expressed my concerns, Lana assured me she was not and asked me to try to put myself in Natalie's shoes.

When I did, I realized that this young woman was betrayed in the worst possible way by two of the people she cared about most. She returned to what was supposed to be the safety of her apartment to find what she thought was her other best friend being sexually assaulted. Then, she finds out that the same best friend is hiding a part of her life, and it's no small part. BDSM is still considered by many to be a deviant or taboo lifestyle. Needless to say, Natalie's struggling to process everything. As difficult as this is, Lana's being a good friend by not shoving me in Natalie's face.

Complicating things on our end is that Svetlana wants to hold off on signing the contract until she returns from Russia. I agreed, but I can't help the lingering disappointment that our dynamic is getting put on hold—again.

"What are you doing here still?" Alex asks when he walks by my office.

"Same thing you're doing here, I suppose."

"Lana's still refusing to leave her roommate?"

"I can't blame her. The girl was terrified."

"I get that," Alex says as he walks into my office and sits across from my desk. "But she's not a fragile flower that's going to wilt and die if she's left alone for a few hours."

"I don't know her roommate." I shrug. "So, I'm following Lana's lead."

"This is a hard time of the year for her."

"That's why I'm not pushing."

"Don't give up on her," Alex encourages me.

Falling for Lana was never in my plans. Little did I know that from the very beginning, my chances of resisting her were slim to none—I never stood a chance. From the first night, an inexplicable addiction took hold. I had to see her again.

While others describe Lana as a strong-willed woman, I see beyond the surface. She's a woman who's braved the darkest depths of what humanity offers. Lana endured horrors that would bring most of us to our knees. Instead of succumbing to hatred and resentment, her compassionate heart remains tender, yearning to alleviate the suffering of others. There is an undeniable feistiness about her, a fiery spirit that ignites my own passions. I wouldn't dare dream of extinguishing that flame because doing so means snuffing out part of what makes Lana so special.

I love Svetlana Solonik. Like the life-sustaining beat of my heart, she's a part of me that I need to survive. Without her, I'm nothing.

Giving up on Svetlana is something I'll never do.

Grayson

DECEMBER 18 SESSION NOTES

Svetlana was visibly anxious when she arrived for her appointment this afternoon. She began the session by telling me about the changes to her upcoming trip to Russia to visit her family. Initially, Brandon was to accompany her, but now her roommate is traveling with her instead.

She expressed apprehension about returning home at this time of the year. Although she won't be there on the anniversary of her sister's abduction, it's still a somber time for her family. *Note- Natalie is not aware that Lana had a sister. Lana's concerned because Natalie lost her brother to suicide several years ago, and she doesn't want to trigger any unpleasant memories.

I suggested that if Svetlana opens up to Natalie about her past, it might be a time of healing for both young women. Svetlana is opposed to that because it will lead to revealing her father's career in the Bratva, which is something she's unwilling to do. I support her reasoning as this is a topic that falls out of the realm of typical.

Svetlana then shifted the conversation to the Dominant/submissive contract she's ready to sign with Brandon—something that was supposed to take place before she went to Russia. She informed me she needed more time, so she postponed this event. I asked how Brandon took the news. She explained he was rightfully disappointed but understanding. I reaffirmed that if she wasn't ready to move forward with the contract, she did the right thing by asking for more time. I also reminded her I'm here if/when she's ready to discuss her reasoning in more detail.

For most of her young adult life, this time of the year is when she chose to retreat both mentally and physically. Svetlana is a unique case and has the ability to disappear with her bodyguard, someone who's known her since childhood. He's always helped her avoid the traumatic memories associated with the anniversary of her sister's abduction. This is something Svetlana has not done for several years. The act of choosing to make a trip home so close to this date marks progress in her healing.

I will be available to her round the clock while she is away due to the increased risk of trauma responses.

Svetlana

ALL THE LAST-MINUTE CHANGES HAVE MADE THIS TRIP home a whirlwind experience. Since my trip no longer includes Brandon, I made plans with Natalie to fly home in time to celebrate Christmas on December 25th since we'll need to be back in New York before Orthodox Christmas.

"We're here," I say and elbow Natalie who fell asleep on the ride here.

Natalie opens her eyes and stretches. "I didn't realize I fell asleep."

The on-duty guard must've been tracking our car via its GPS locator because the gates are already opening before Misha makes it to the guard station.

"Svetlana," she says and grabs my arm. "I've never seen anything so beautiful."

Papa mentioned he was having the house decorated for Natalie so she wouldn't feel like she missed out on celebrating the holiday. But I had no idea he was doing all this.

A breathtaking scene unfolds before us. Luminary candles line the path, casting an inviting glow that dances in the gentle breeze. Each flickering flame creates a mesmerizing display that captures the enchantment of the holiday season. The surrounding trees are adorned with strings of clear twinkling lights that only add to the magic.

When our house comes into view, even my breath catches. Softly shimmering lights embellish every nook and cranny, delicately tracing the edges of our home with a whimsical radiance. In each window is a candle. Their warm glow illuminates each space with a cozy ambiance.

As if nature herself was in on Papa's plans, snow begins to fall. Each flake glistens in the glow of the lights. The air is filled with an undeniable aura of joy and anticipation, as if everything around us hums with excitement.

Misha pulls the car to a stop, and Natalie jumps out. She twirls around with her mittened hands outstretched. "I feel like I'm in a life-sized snow globe," she giggles.

"I think it's more like one of those Hallmark Christmas movies you girls force me to watch," Pyotr says.

"The ones that always make you teary," I joke.

Misha looks at him. "You cry at movies now? Has living abroad made you soft?"

"I'm afraid my little butterfly is so exhausted she has no idea what she's talking about." Pyotr looks at Natalie, who's watching the interaction cautiously, and winks. "Natalie will tell you. I watch them under duress."

"He hates them." She corroborates his story.

"Sure," Misha laughs as he walks past with some of our bags in tow.

"I knew I liked you," Pyotr says, making Natalie smile bigger. He grabs the rest of our bags while I explore some of the lights with Natalie.

"Did you know about this?"

"Kind of." I smile. "Papa mentioned he was going to do some decorating. I should've known he'd go all out."

"I thought I heard a car," Mama says as she steps outside. "How long have you been out here?"

"Only a few minutes." I walk over to her and give her a hug.

"It's so good to have you home. I've missed you so much."

"It's only been a few months."

"It feels like longer to me. Welcome home, Natalie," Mama says, wrapping her in a hug.

"Thank you, Irina," Natalie says hesitantly. "I was excited when Lana asked me to come home with her."

"I thought I heard my girls," Papa says, appearing in the doorway. "The three of you need to get inside before you catch a cold."

"Maxim," Natalie says quietly, "The decorations are beautiful."

"I was hoping you would like them." He smiles.

"They're perfect."

I was afraid that coming home this time of the year would feel suffocating with sorrow. Instead, the combination of holiday decorations and the softly falling snow transports us to a realm where dreams come true, and the spirit of the season fills our hearts with warmth and joy. And it doesn't stop outside.

Walking into the house feels like stepping foot inside a Christmas wonderland. The staircase inside the foyer is adorned with lighted evergreen garlands. Holiday trees decorate the entrance, and our antique nativity is on full display. I don't know where to look first.

"Are you girls hungry?" Mama asks. "I can have Olga prepare a snack."

I look at Natalie, who shakes her head. "I think we're going to get settled in and try to get some sleep."

"Your rooms are ready for you," Mama says. "It's so good to have you girls home."

We celebrate Christmas morning, exchanging gifts by a tree that's easily ten feet tall. It's something we've never done before, at least not like this. Despite being fully grown, I can't help the childlike excitement that takes over as I tear the paper off my presents.

Papa and Mama shower both Natalie and me with clothes, jewelry, and gift cards for our favorite stores in New York.

"Thank you both so very much," Natalie says when we've finished opening the gifts.

"You are very welcome, Natalia," Papa answers with a smile. "Having you and *moya babochka* here has been good for the heart."

"I wasn't looking forward to this holiday," she says sadly. "After everything that happened with Tommy."

"That young man was not deserving of you," Mama adds.

"We are not talking about him today," Papa says. "Today is for celebrating."

Unfortunately, our trip home is not long enough, and before I know it, we're back on Papa's jet, returning to New York.

I hate not being here with my family through this difficult time. Celebrating Christmas with Natalie took what's always been dreaded days and infused them with joy. It feels like a new beginning. Hopefully, this is a tradition we can continue.

Grayson

MAY 13 SESSION NOTES

Svetlana has regularly attended sessions every two weeks over the past few months. There were many difficult weeks as she faced the memory of the events leading up to her sister's murder. On the anniversary of Jelena's death, I accompanied her to Central Park, where we released a single white balloon that carried a note Svetlana wrote to her sister. It was an emotional moment for both of us. I'm proud of Svetlana for not running from her memories as she's done in the past.

She's still seeing Brandon but has yet to sign a Dom/sub contract with him. Svetlana is open about having feelings for Brandon outside of any dynamic. However, she refuses to address why she's putting off signing the contract. I suspect she fears the commitment that comes with a contractual relationship. Something Svetlana denies.

Svetlana expressed excitement about the completion of her first year of law school. Because she's in an accelerated program, she'll only have one more year of study to be eligible to sit for the bar exam. Her work ethic is second to none, and for that, I have to commend her.

We will be continuing sessions over the summer months as she plans to remain in the United States and will be interning at a law firm in Manhattan.

Grayson

SEPTEMBER 7 SESSION NOTES

This is the first in-person session Svetlana and I have had since July. She has kept in touch via text, but because of some last-minute travel during her summer break, she could not attend in-person sessions. Despite not meeting in the office, Svetlana continues working on her treatment goals.

School's back in full swing, and Svetlana reports being happy with her courses. She's said for some time that she's experiencing anxiety concerning school, interning, and her personal life. I've suggested different coping mechanisms I thought might be helpful. Despite her efforts, none of them seemed to be beneficial.

Given her history of running and secluding, I was concerned. I was pleasantly surprised when she informed me that while she was in Russia, she visited the school where she took ballet as a child.

I was unaware until this time that Svetlana took ballet lessons as a young girl. She reports that it was something she loved but gave up in her teens. Svetlana describes stepping into the studio as feeling like being home. When she returned to Manhattan, she found a ballet school and has attended several classes.

Svetlana explained dance has provided her with an outlet for the emotions she otherwise bottles up. I expressed how proud I am of her for admitting she was struggling and also for finding a coping mechanism that is healthy and effective.

My recent observations correlate with her self-reports. Svetlana's much more settled—at peace. I'm hopeful that this represents a turning point in her healing journey.

The subject of Brandon and their unsigned contract was revisited. Although they two have been seeing one another more over the summer, coupled with the fact that Natalie's expressed an interest in getting to know him, Svetlana still keeps them separate.

Svetlana explained she's been doing a great deal of soul-searching regarding the unsigned contract. She acknowledges that her fear of commitment has been a significant deterrent and reason for her not signing. I suggested the possibility of a shorter-term contract—baby steps, if you will. Svetlana was not opposed to that idea and said she'd consider bringing that idea to Brandon.

Once again, I reminded her about the importance of honest communication in the BDSM lifestyle. I encouraged her to talk to Brandon about her fears. Adding that if they're going to be a Dominant/submissive couple, she must allow herself to trust him. It's an idea she seems to be warming up to.

As it was time for our regular evaluation, I asked Svetlana for her opinion about our sessions. She feels therapy has been helpful and is beginning to see progress. We're in agreement to continue our therapeutic relationship.

Svetlana

THREE YEARS. THAT'S HOW LONG IT'S TAKEN TO GET TO this moment, but we're finally here. Brandon's picking me up from Alex's apartment, and then we're going to Fire and Ice, where we'll sign our contract. It's been a lesson in patience and understanding for each of us as we waded through the murky waters of our pasts.

Brandon's already proved himself as a capable Dominant. He's been my safe place while I've been learning how to better regulate my emotions and face my insecurities. After this process, I have a better understanding of why a prospective couple shouldn't be intimately involved. It creates a messy and confusing situation—one I wouldn't suggest to anyone. However, I stand by the decision Brandon and I made for us.

While I do my make-up, I think back to that night in the private room at the club. I thought I was ready to submit to a Dominant and was sure Brandon would offer me a contract and suggest we start vetting. Instead, he asked for more time.

Initially, I was disappointed. I thought if I told him I was okay with going slow, it would only be a few weeks, a month or two tops, before we took the next step. Days turned into weeks, into months, into years.

And then the tables turned. This time, Brandon was ready, but it was me holding back. At times, it seemed we'd never get on the same page. But finally, after a lot of serious negotiations, we made it.

"Lana," Alex calls as he knocks on the door. "Brandon's here."

"I'll be right out." I twirl in front of the full-length mirror, ensuring everything is perfect. When I was shopping, I couldn't make up my mind. So, I bought three outfits for tonight. I've gone back and forth all day before settling on a simple white strapless mini-dress that dips slightly on my back. I've paired it with five-inch white stilettos that tie around my calves. Once I'm satisfied with my appearance, I shut the lights off and follow the sound of the guys' voices to the kitchen.

Alex stops speaking mid-sentence when he sees me standing in the doorway. He motions with his chin for Brandon, whose back is to me, to turn around.

"Holy—" He swipes his hand over his head. "You look fucking incredible."

"I think I'll leave you kids alone," Alex says.

"Aren't you coming to the club tonight?" I ask.

"No. I'm staying in."

"You really need to get out more," Brandon says.

"I get out plenty. You two have fun." Alex takes his bottle of water and leaves Brandon and me alone.

"I'm a little worried about him," Brandon says after Alex leaves the room. "All he does is work."

I've been concerned about Alex, too. But I didn't think it was my place to say anything because, let's face it, all my ducks aren't exactly lined up.

"I wish he'd be more open to a submissive. Star's had so many girls approach her asking about him, but he refuses to even consider it," Brandon explains.

"You don't have to tell me. I hear about it all the time. They think because we're friends, I can somehow get Alex to pay attention to them." I roll my eyes, annoyed at the thought.

"Hopefully, he'll come around." Brandon takes my hand. "We need to leave, or we'll be late."

"Late for what?"

"I made reservations for dinner," Brandon says on the elevator ride to the parking garage.

"I thought we were going to the club?"

"I changed the plan. Tonight's a special night."

"Do I get to know where we're going?" I ask as we walk to where he's parked.

"Nope." Brandon opens the car door and helps me in.

After a drive across town, Brandon pulls up to valet parking at Torch, an exclusive restaurant in Brooklyn.

"I'm afraid I didn't dress appropriately for a restaurant," I say as I get out of the car and link my hand with Brandon's.

"You look good to me." His hungry gaze travels up and down my body. "But you won't have to worry. No one will see you."

"What do you mean?"

"You'll see," Brandon smirks.

We're escorted into a dark room and seated at a table for two. I hear the soft murmurings of what I assume are other diners, but it takes my eyes a few seconds to adjust before I can make out the shapes.

"I'm going to put your blindfold on now," the server says before tying a piece of silk over my eyes.

"Brandon, what's going on?" I ask quietly when I'm certain the server is no longer at our table.

"This restaurant offers an immersive dining experience. We'll remain blindfolded while our meal is served."

I've never heard of such a thing, but over the next hour and a half, we're treated to a dining experience unlike anything I've ever had. A fruity wine that tastes like peach and apricot is served with an appetizer that's meant to be eaten with our hands. I find what feels like a small piece of toasted bread. I put it in my mouth, and an explosion of flavors assaults my senses. The toast had a subtle garlic flavor. Topping it is a sweet and creamy ricotta cheese and fiery honey. Together, this dish is divine.

The main course is set before us. With my vision restricted, my other senses are on high alert. The aroma is unfamiliar except for the smell of basil. Taking my fork, I try to get some of all the ingredients I feel in the bowl onto it. The food hits my tongue, and I'm overwhelmed by the unfamiliar flavors. The tomato sauce has a hint of spice, giving it a slight bit of heat, and the pasta is rich and nutty. The next bite contains another flavor I'm not accustomed to. It's tender and has earthy notes.

"What is this?"

"I think it might be eggplant," Brandon answers.

I'm familiar with eggplant from a dish, *Ikra,* lovingly known as Eggplant caviar. But in that dish, the eggplant is pureed with peppers, garlic, and tomatoes and served as a cold appetizer. I've never had it prepared like this.

"Do you like it?" he asks.

"It's yummy." I take another bite. "I'd love to learn how to cook eggplant like this."

"We can ask Tony if he can teach you this dish," Brandon suggests.

"Do you think he'd mind?"

"Not at all."

Paired with the main course is red wine. The fragrance has aromas of cherry and roses. The taste is earthy yet has fruity undertones. I hope after the meal, we get to know what everything we're trying is.

Dessert is served in what feels like a coffee cup. We're instructed to use our spoon for the dessert portion and then to drink the remainder, which I can already tell is coffee. When the spoon hits my tongue, I recognize it as ice cream with subtle hints of chocolate. After I finish the ice cream, I take a sip of what can only be a rich Italian espresso.

Just as I'd hoped, after the meal, we're instructed to remove the blindfolds. The lights in the room are turned to a dim setting. Our server hands us each a copy of the menu from this evening's meal.

"Thank you," I say to Brandon as we leave the restaurant. "That was the most unique dining experience I've ever had."

"I'm glad you enjoyed it."

"Where to now?"

"We're going to my house. There's a contract waiting to be signed."

A surge of excitement courses through my veins as my heart rate kicks into high gear, knowing tonight will not end before we're finally Dominant and submissive.

Brandon

I GRIP THE STEERING WHEEL TIGHTLY, TRYING TO MASK the trembling in my hands. We've just had an incredible dining experience that far exceeded my expectations. Now, Lana and I are on our way back to my house, where we'll finally sign the contract. If all goes as planned, I'll have her gagged and tied to my bed shortly.

Luck is in my favor because we hit all green lights. I pull the Mustang into my driveway and kill the engine. Turning slightly in my seat, I say. "Are you ready?"

"I am."

Before I left the house, I set out the papers and pens on my dining room table. I didn't want to waste any time once we got here. I usher Lana into the room and pull the seat out for her. "Can I get you anything to drink?"

"A glass of ice water would be wonderful."

When my parents passed away, their house was left to me. The house is more traditional in style, with a formal dining area that's separate from the kitchen. My plan is to eventually knock out the walls and have a modern open floor plan. Because I work so much, I haven't had much time to do any updates.

I leave Lana and go get our drinks. My anxiety's out of

control. So, I take my time, ensuring I'm calm and centered before returning to Lana and setting the glass on the table.

"Thank you." Svetlana looks up. Her blue eyes remind me of the sky on a cloudless day. If she's nervous, she's hiding it well.

I sit across from her and sip my water before setting it down. Pulling the papers closer to me, I look at Lana. "I'd like for us to review the contract a final time to ensure all the requested changes were made correctly and that we're both in agreement with moving forward."

Her mood shifts to serious and business-like. "I appreciate that."

We start on page one and take it line by line. It may be overkill, but this is important, and I want to be sure that every detail has been covered. Mistakes can be made too easily, and I'm not leaving anything to chance. Svetlana shows no signs of impatience as I read aloud.

"I added the time limit of one year as promised. With the agreement that we'll review the contract at that time," I add.

"That's perfect. Thank you."

Finally, we reach the last page. At the bottom are two blank lines where we'll sign our names, solidifying our agreement and the beginning of the contract.

"Before we sign, there's something I need to say."

"Okay," Lana says hesitantly.

"Contract or no contract, I've fallen for you." I get up and walk over to where she sits. "I'm excited about what's on those pages, but I want so much more. I love you, Svetlana."

She looks up, meeting my gaze. "I love you, too."

I lean down and brush my lips against hers. "We need to sign this because I don't want to wait another second to take you to bed."

Lana giggles and then picks up her pen, signing her name. She holds it out for me, and I do the same. With that one small move, the remaining walls between us finally crumble.

She rises from her chair and asks, "What now?" Lana bites her bottom lip.

The look on her face makes me lose the last shred of self-control. I swipe my hand across the table, causing papers to fly through the air. Our water glasses smash off the hardwood floor, but I don't care. Reaching behind her, I unzip her dress and watch as she shimmies it down her legs. She steps out of the pile of fabric, and I kick it aside. I'm not surprised to find her bare underneath.

"Lay on the table and open your legs." My voice is low and commanding. She obeys without hesitation. "You're so wet already," I say as I drag my finger along her slit.

Unzipping my pants, I free my hard cock. "Who do you belong to?"

"I belong to you, Sir."

I pull her to the edge of the table. My hands grip her hips as I tease her with the tip of my cock. Her hips lift from the table, and I stop. Lana groans at the loss of contact.

"I'm the only man who'll ever touch this pussy again."

"You're the only man I ever want to touch me. The only one I want to feel inside me. It'll always be you."

I didn't know how badly I needed to hear someone say that I'm their everything. Hearing Svetlana say those words healed fissures in my heart that I didn't realize were still there. For the first time in so long, I feel completely whole.

With one hand on her hip, I line myself up with her opening and enter her. Lana's breath catches. "You feel so fucking good. Like you were made for me."

"Mmm," she responds.

I start moving slowly at first. Her hands move to her breasts, kneading the flesh and twisting her nipples between her fingers. Gripping her hips, I increase my pace. One of my hands goes between her legs, rubbing fast, hard circles on her clit. I need her to come with me. To solidify our words with our bodies.

I don't have to ask. I know from her panting breaths and the tensing of her body that she's close. Her orgasm begins a second before mine. The quick pulsing of her body around my cock triggers my own pleasure. The significance of this shared moment, the joining of our bodies and the beginning of our dynamic, only makes me come harder.

Once our bodies still, I ask, "Are you okay?"

Lana pushes up on her elbows. "Yes, I am. But I don't think your dining room is."

"I don't give a fuck about my dining room." I pull out and help her up.

"Where do you keep your broom? I'll clean up the broken glass."

"I'll get it later."

"Don't be silly," she says. "It'll only take a minute."

"Are you arguing with me already?"

"Maybe," she says coyly.

"I have a cure for that."

"You do?"

"Yes." I toss her over my shoulder, earning a squeal. "There's a ball gag in my room with your name on it."

Svetlana

Since the night Natalie walked in on her ex-boyfriend in bed with her ex-best friend and then walked in on Brandon and me, she's been making a lot of changes in her life. No longer is she the timid girl from a small town who lets everyone walk all over her. She's much more confident and has even gone out with me on several weekends.

Still, I haven't figured out how to tell Natalie about tonight. I've tried so many times but backed out at the last second. Now, I'm out of time. What I'm about to ask will be a big stretch, though, and I'm terrified.

"Are you still studying?" I snatch the textbook from her hand and read the title aloud, "Love and Attachment: Adult Relationships." I do my best to hold in a laugh. "You need to get out of this apartment."

"I have a paper." Natalie jumps off the couch and swipes at the book. I'm several inches taller than her and easily hold it out of reach.

"You can study tomorrow. Tonight, I want you to come out with me."

"But—"

"Come on, Nat." I give in and return the book.

Natalie takes it and sits back on the sofa, quickly flipping through the pages to find her place. "I'll go out next weekend, I promise."

"I need you to come out tonight." I drop down on the sofa next to her.

"Why?"

Here goes nothing. "Well, you remember Brandon, the guy you called the cops on?" I hold back the laugh that's threatening to escape.

Natalie's cheeks turn bright red. "How could I forget."

"Thankfully, you didn't scare him away."

"That's good because he sure is hot."

"He is, isn't he." I can't help the smile that spreads across my face. "I've finally consented to be his submissive," I say and gauge Natalie's response before continuing, "We're doing a scene at the club tonight, and I really want you there."

Natalie's eyes widen, and she closes the book giving me her full attention.

"You're doing a scene? Like getting naked in front of an audience?"

I nod slowly, hoping I haven't totally freaked her out. I don't want her to lose all the ground she's gained.

"This is what you want?" she asks, uncertain.

I'm scared to admit how much I want this. "I'm so excited about it, but please, I need my best friend there."

"I wouldn't miss it for the world," Natalie squeals and pulls me in for a tight hug.

Her reaction is unexpected. "I'm so glad you said yes. You're going to have a great time."

The look on her face tells me she's not convinced, but I have a plan up my sleeve that will hopefully make this the best night of her life.

I'm even happier when Natalie puts her books aside and spends the day primping for tonight. We spend the rest of the afternoon giving each other mani/pedis before I shower. When I come out, Natalie's waiting to fix my hair.

Brandon and I are doing a very intense scene tonight, and I need my hair up and out of the way. Fortunately, Natalie is great at fixing hair, so I let her have free reign. She starts with a fishtail that transitions into a beautiful tight bun.

"There. All done," she says after putting in the last pin.

I hold up an extra mirror to see the back of my hair. "Thanks, I love it."

"I need to jump in the shower quick and find something to wear," Natalie says as she leaves my room. "What do you suggest I wear tonight?" she asks from my doorway, startling me.

"I was hoping you'd ask. I have the perfect outfit for you." I hurry into my closet to grab the dress I put aside for her.

Natalie lets out a huff. "You're kidding, right?"

I knew this part might be a fight, but I'm far more stubborn than she is. "Nat, you're gorgeous." I push the hanger into her hands. "You're going to turn heads tonight."

"Do I want to turn heads?"

"You never know who you might meet." I point Natalie in the direction of her room and give her an encouraging nudge forward. "Go shower and get dressed. Now."

"Are you sure you're not a Domme?" She laughs as she walks down the hall to her room. "You're awfully bossy." Several moments later, Natalie yells down the hall again. "How do I wear a bra with this thing?"

"You don't." It's my turn to laugh this time.

I get dressed and start my makeup when I get a text.

Brandon: Are you ready for tonight?

Me: I'm finishing up right now, Sir.

Brandon: Good. I'll be waiting for you at the club, *mon petit papillon.*

A shiver of excitement runs down my spine. I knew from the first time I met Brandon, when Alex brought him home for dinner, that if I was given the chance, I'd agree to submit to him. He's everything I've always wanted in a Dominant—even some things I didn't know I wanted. This is the first scene Brandon and I are doing as an official Dominant/submissive couple. We've been doing scenes for several years, but nothing like what we've planned for tonight and certainly nothing in public.

At first, Brandon wasn't sold on the idea of a public scene. Although he'd never admit it, what happened years ago with Celia still haunts him. One of the main sticking points in our contract is that he's unwilling to share me—ever. It's something I wasn't necessarily looking for, but I'm not opposed to it, either. It was so important to him, so I agreed to it. But I never agreed to not doing public scenes.

We've been going back and forth about it for a few weeks. He even brought Star into the conversations. Once he was confident there'd be no one else involved and that Star would have security on hand specifically for our scene, he agreed. I'm so excited he did.

I finish my makeup and go to Natalie's room to see if she's ready. I find her checking herself out in the mirror. "I knew it! You look amazing!" Natalie turns around and wraps her arms around my neck.

"What should I expect tonight?" she asks, suddenly looking nervous.

"The car's here. I'll tell you on the way."

"The car?"

"Brandon sent a car to pick us up. You ready?"

"Yep. Don't want to keep your man waiting."

Brandon

WHAT THE HELL DID I AGREE TO THIS FOR? HOW DID I let Svetlana talk me into a public scene? I would never have agreed to this if it wasn't for Star's intervention.

But I know this club. It's not like Chains. The people here are strictly vetted. Star and Owen have detailed plans for every public scene in Fire and Ice. They'd never let what happened to Celia happen in their club. Although I know all this, I'm still nervous.

As if all that wasn't enough, Svetlana approached me earlier this week with another of her crazy ideas. She wants to set Alex and Natalie up. I have to admit at first, I wasn't on board. I mean, this is the same girl who called 911 on me last year. I haven't seen her since that night, but Lana says Natalie's different. She's opened up to a lot of new ideas and has even shown an interested in BDSM.

And then there's Alex. He's been single for more years than I can count. Alex says he's not interested in a relationship, but if things don't change, he's going to work himself into an early grave. So, I agreed to help Lana get them together.

I pull up Alex's contact on my cell and send him a text.

Me: Remember Lana's roommate?

Alex: Yes...

Me: She's coming to the club tonight. I need a favor.

Alex: No.

I'm choosing to ignore his protests.

Me: She needs an escort.

Alex: The same girl who called the cops on you last year?

Now, I kind of regret telling him about that because it's only going to make getting him to say yes more difficult.

Me: Yeah.

Alex: And you want me to escort her?

Me: Come on, bro.

There's a long pause, and I know it's because he's trying to find a way to get out of this.

Me: You know I'd do it for you.

Alex: I'm not feeling well. I don't think I can make it.

Me: The fuck you aren't. You're out running right now. Tell me I'm wrong.

Alex: Fine. But you owe me.

Me: Thanks, man.

Step one is complete. Now, we cross our fingers and hope they hit it off.

Svetlana

ON THE RIDE TO THE CLUB, I TRY TO TELL NATALIE AS much as possible about what to expect at Fire and Ice tonight. She asks a lot of follow-up questions, and although I do my best to answer her, I know she won't fully understand until she sees it for herself. I think she's going to be surprised. The club isn't anything like what I know she's imagining it to be.

Brandon's driver pulls the car to a stop in front of the building. When we get out of the car, Natalie looks around. "Is Pyotr here?"

"I'm sure he's around somewhere." I know he's lurking in the shadows, keeping a watchful eye on me, but he's no longer a significant presence in my life. The closer Brandon and I get, the more distant Pyotr gets. When I asked him about it, he said it's because I don't need him as much now that I have Brandon. Part of me is thankful for the space and freedom, but the other part misses the man who's been by my side since I was a little girl.

The bouncer opens the club's door when he sees us approach. We step into the foyer, which is already busy. Master Kyoshi, a Shibari expert, will be doing a scene tonight. I'm sure that's why everyone's here so early. But unless they're helping set up or are in one of the scenes, they'll be waiting out here for a while.

There are several people in line ahead of us checking in. While we wait, Natalie tugs at her dress.

"Stop fidgeting," I say, and I feel like a mother hen.

"I'm so nervous, but I'm also excited. Is that normal?"

"It's perfectly normal. Don't worry." I squeeze her hand. "We're going to have a great time tonight. When we get to the desk, you'll be checked in as my guest. Mistress Star will give you a colored wristband."

"What's it for?"

"The colors represent a person's availability." I point to the sign on the wall that explains the color system. It's based on a rainbow where each color represents whether a guest is a Dominant or submissive, with a partner or alone, just watching or looking to play.

"You'll get a purple band. It means you're being sponsored by a Dominant, and no one can approach you without asking his permission first." It's our turn to check in, so I approach the counter. "Good evening, Lana."

"Good evening, Mistress. This is my friend, Natalie." I motion next to me. "She'll be our guest this evening."

"Brandon gave me her information." Mistress Star looks at Natalie. "Has Lana explained our color system?"

"Yes, she has."

"Do you have any questions?"

"No," Natalie says quietly.

"May I have your right arm?" Natalie holds it out, and Star puts the wristband on. "You understand you'll have a Dominant responsible for your comfort and safety tonight?"

"I do."

"Are you comfortable with that?" Star asks.

One of Natalie's concerns was if the club took consent seriously. She was online and read some horror stories. Natalie doesn't know about Brandon's past. It's not my story to tell. I assured her neither Brandon nor I would be members at a club where safe and consensual play wasn't enforced.

"Yes, ma'am."

"You ladies can go right in. Brandon is waiting for you by stage three," Mistress Star instructs. "Natalie, I hope you have a wonderful evening. I'll be around all night if you have any questions or concerns."

We're fully checked in. This is it. I grab Natalie by the arm and nearly drag her through the large medieval-looking doors that lead into the club. "Come on. I'm so excited for you to officially meet Brandon."

Natalie steps into the room before me and freezes as she looks around the room. She says nothing, leaving me to wonder what's going through her mind.

Fire and Ice is an upscale club with a modern industrial vibe. The main room, where we're standing, is where all the public scenes occur. Currently, the bright overhead lighting is on. Later, the professional stage lights will help to set the mood for each scene.

"Things don't start for a few hours. That's when the real fun happens." I wiggle my eyebrows, trying to break the tension. Feeling more confident that Natalie's okay, I look for Brandon and motion for Natalie to come with me. Without me saying anything, he turns around and gives me a look that makes my insides quiver. "Natalie, I'd like you to meet my Dominant, Brandon."

"It's nice to meet you." Brandon offers her a kind smile.

Natalie's cheeks turn pink as she says, "It's nice to meet you too. I'm sorry for calling the police."

"Already forgiven. It's good to know Lana has someone looking out for her."

The sound of creaky wheels steals Natalie's attention. On the stage, two of the club's members are moving a black walnut St. Andrew's cross onto the stage. Once it's in place, the only sound remaining is from the metal cuffs banging against the wood.

"What's that thing? It looks like a torture device."

Brandon laughs. "It's a Saint Andrew's Cross. I'll secure Lana to it and use my whip to pleasure her."

Natalie's brow furrows. "Your whip? Won't that hurt her?"

"I won't her hurt—much." He winks.

Natalie looks at me, her eyes full of concern. I don't have a chance to respond before Brandon explains, "Lana likes pain, and I know how to give her what she craves without hurting her." He attempts to reassure her, but she doesn't seem convinced.

"It's okay, Nat. Brandon and I have already talked about everything we'll do tonight. This is something I want."

"You're sure?" she asks, clearly not believing me.

"Positive."

Brandon looks over Natalie's shoulder, and a grin spreads across his face. Natalie spins around, and I know the exact second she sees him. Alex has just walked in and is standing across the room. He runs his hand through his dark hair and looks around. As soon as he sees Brandon, he smiles and starts walking our way.

It never ceases to amaze me how both men and women fall all over themselves when Alex enters a room. The other submissives always carry on about how hot he is. They think I'm crazy when I don't join them, making up fantasies about him. When I look at him, all I see is Alex, the guy I've known for years. The one who, most times, makes me want to scream and pull *his* hair out.

What's most important is that Natalie seems to have fallen under his spell. And Brandon didn't want me playing matchmaker.

"Glad you made it," Brandon says as he shakes Alex's hand.

"I wouldn't miss it." He turns to me, and from the amused look on his face, I know he realizes I'm behind this little setup. "How are you tonight, Svetlana?"

"I'm fine, thank you," I answer and, like a well-trained submissive, keep my gaze cast down. Well, that and I don't want to fight with Alex right now.

Thankfully, Brandon steps in. "Natalie. I want to introduce you to my best friend, Alex." She remains quiet, her eyes fixed on the man across from her. "Alex is also a Dominant here. I've asked him to be your escort in my absence tonight."

"Oh," she says. "I thought I'd be staying with you and Lana?" Natalie looks at me, and I shrug, feigning innocence. If all goes well, she'll thank me later.

"We won't be available for the entire evening, and because you're a first-time guest, you can't be alone in the club," Brandon explains. "You're in good hands with Alex."

"I've heard a lot about you." Alex tries to hold back a smirk.

"You have?" Natalie turns to me, but I slink behind Brandon.

"I have. You're the girl who called the police on my friend here." Alex smiles and slaps Brandon on the back.

"Oh, my God. I can't believe you told anyone about that." If I thought Natalie's cheeks were red when I introduced her to Brandon, I was wrong. Right now, they are flaming from a mix of embarrassment and fury.

"There's no reason to be embarrassed. I'm sure Brandon appreciated your desire to protect your roommate," Alex chuckles.

"Lana and I have to finish setting up our stage," Brandon interrupts. "We'll see you two later."

I give Nat a small wave as I walk away with Brandon, leaving Alex and her alone. "Do you think they're going to get along?"

"Maybe." Brandon shrugs.

"What do you mean, maybe? They're both unattached. And did you see how they couldn't take their eyes off each other?"

Without warning, Brandon stops, and I nearly collide with his back. "Svetlana, I do not like you playing matchmaker with our friends."

"But you agreed—"

"I agreed to ask Alex to come tonight to sit with Natalie because she's your friend, and I don't want her being paired with someone I don't know. But that's as far as I'm willing to go."

"But—"

"No more buts. After tonight, that's it. I won't be a part of trying to get them together." He starts walking again. "And neither will you."

"Yes, Sir."

If everything goes according to plan, they won't need our intervention after tonight.

Brandon and I spend a few minutes together before our scene. He reserved a private room, so we have a quiet place for aftercare. Providing aftercare is the responsible thing to do following BDSM play, but Brandon places extra focus on it because of my traumatic past.

With my permission, Brandon met with Gray several times to discuss his concerns. He wanted to be sure he had every resource on hand to help me recover physically and emotionally from a scene. Especially tonight's. It's going to be intense and will challenge each of us.

"Are you sure you're ready for this?" Brandon asks when I exit the ensuite in my black silk robe.

"I'm positive," I say, closing the distance between us. "Are you still on board with it?"

"I am." He pulls me against him.

His grey eyes have a faraway look. "What's wrong?"

"I know the damage a whip can do. I don't—"

"You aren't going to hurt me." Brandon doesn't react. "May I speak freely?"

"Of course."

"Celia was not injured by your hand. I know you don't like to hear it, but you both were victims that night. If you weren't drugged, you would've never let any harm come to Celia, just like you'll never allow me to be hurt." He tries to turn away, but I use my hand to direct him back to me. "I trust you, Sir."

"I'll protect you with my life, *mon petit papillon.*" His lips meet mine, and he kisses me. It starts slowly and gently. Then, he grabs the back of my neck and deepens the kiss. His other hand slides down my front. He fumbles with the belt, holding my robe closed. Brandon groans, "We need to stop before I decide to fuck you instead."

"We'll be back in here after the scene. We can pick up where we're leaving off then."

"Not at the club."

We've had sex at the club once—in the school role-playing room. That was the one and only time Brandon let his guard down. Since then, he has refused to have sex here.

"Can't blame a girl for trying." I smile.

He steps back, putting a few inches of space between us. "It's time to go."

Brandon

WHEN I OPEN THE DOOR, THE MUSIC FROM THE CLUB'S main room floods in. Part of me wishes I had the courage to pull Lana back inside to finish what we started. The other part thrums with excitement for what we're about to do.

I've spent years learning and practicing with a whip. I'm confident in my skills, but that doesn't stop memories from creeping into the forefront of my mind. But this time, I'm older and more experienced. We're in a reputable club. Star has extra security in place to help me feel more comfortable with a public scene. I've also worked closely with Grayson to ensure I can properly care for Lana when the scene ends.

With Lana's hand in mine, we step into the main room. The music stops, and the noise in the club lowers to a soft murmur as we step onto the platform. Lana turns and faces me. I nod, her cue to begin. With ease, she unties the belt, and her robe flutters open, exposing her breasts and neatly groomed pussy. Reaching out, I slide the silky fabric down her arms and set it on a table that's positioned off to the side.

When I return to Svetlana, I pause, needing to take a deep breath. Lana stands facing the club filled with people, most of whom are gathered in front of our stage. She's completely nude yet shows no signs of nerves or insecurity. Instead, her arms hang loosely at her sides, and her head is lowered. I'm in awe of the poise she's demonstrating.

I walk back to her and run my knuckles down her cheek. "What are your safe words?"

"Red and yellow," she answers.

"I know we agreed on a gag, but I'm eliminating that. I don't feel comfortable."

"Yes, Sir."

I hold my hand out, and she threads her fingers with mine. Together, we approach the X. Lana stands against it and raises her hands above her head. Taking one hand, I wrap the leather restraint around it and secure it tightly before doing the same to the next. "Do they feel okay?"

Lana gives them a tug before answering, "They feel good."

Lowering to my knees, I take her first ankle and secure it in the same fashion as her wrists. Then, I do the same with her left ankle. "Are they too tight?"

"No, Sir."

I take a deep breath and turn toward the main room. I raise my hand to let Jim, our tech person who controls the lighting and music, know I'm ready. The lights in the club dim, and "Cult of Personality" by Living Colour begins playing.

Movement in the crowd catches my attention. Alex and Natalie are taking their place to watch. I pause and look at my best friend, who nods, offering me his silent support. Then, I face Lana, ready to give my undivided attention to our scene.

I lift my bullwhip from its resting place and take several practice swings to warm up my arm. It only takes a few minutes before I hit my stride, and I crack my whip—my signature move signaling I'm starting.

With a flick of my wrist, the thong makes its first contact with Lana's body. My intent with these first few licks of the thong is to warm up her skin and get her used to the stinging sensation. Her body remains relaxed.

Carefully, I work her up to the next level. Each point of impact stings but is still well below where I know her pain threshold typically lies. The extra adrenaline coursing through her system makes tonight's scene more of a balancing act. Lana's less likely to feel pain in the same way she usually does. Because of that, I need to be more aware of any minute reactions she has.

My goal isn't to injure her or cause her any unpleasant pain. I'm turned on each time the leather caresses her skin. I take pleasure in seeing her pale skin turn a stunning shade of red. Her cries are a mix of pain and pleasure. As much as Lana craves pain, I ache to give it to her.

This scene goes beyond eroticism. Lana carries scars from her traumatic past. She's overcome so much, but what happened to Jelena will always be a part of her. As a way to compensate for the helplessness she felt when Jelena was ripped away from her, Lana takes control in every situation she can. That's a heavy weight for anyone to carry.

Tonight, Svetlana is willingly submitting to me. She trusts I'll give her the pain she craves without going too far.

I alternate the intensity and frequency of each lash, ensuring I don't fall into a predictable rhythm as I make a crisscross pattern across her back. When I see her tensing in anticipation, I know it's time to stop and check in with my sub.

Lana's dripping with sweat, and I suspect arousal. Reaching out, I tuck a loose strand of hair behind her ear. "What's your color, *mon petit papillon?*" I whisper.

She pauses before answering, "Green."

Using my thumbs, I tenderly wipe the tears cascading down her cheeks. "You look so fucking gorgeous right now." I feather kisses on her neck. "If we're going to keep going, you need to stop holding your breath. I want you to relax into each strike. Let everything else go. It's just you and me."

"Yes, Sir," she whispers.

"I'm going to start again now."

Lana closes her eyes and takes a deep breath, letting it out slowly. Her body relaxes, and I feel confident about continuing.

With the leather-covered handle firmly in my grasp, I resume the scene with three lashes in quick succession. The crack of the whip echoes in the expansive space. Lana's returned to a relaxed state, so I challenge her with the intensity of the strikes. I will not push her past the agreed-upon boundaries, but I will bring her to a place where she releases everything she clings to.

When Lana's hands relax in their restraints, I know she's nearing the end. I begin to bring down the intensity. As soon as her whimpers silence, I know she's reached subspace, and the scene is over.

I set the whip on the table and stand behind my submissive, running my fingers gently over the marks I left on her. None of them broke her skin, but when she looks at her back in the mirror, she'll have a visual reminder of tonight. Once her aftercare is done, I'll take pictures for her.

Then, I stoop down and begin unfastening her ankle restraints. "You did so well, *mon petit papillon,*" I say quietly as I stand and release her wrists. When Lana goes to subspace, she's unable to speak, but I know she hears me. "You were strong and so beautiful." I cradle her in my arms, and she curls against my chest.

This moment is one I'll cherish—my submissive finding solace and comfort in my embrace.

Svetlana

THE CRACKING SOUND FILLS THE AIR FOR A FRACTION of a second before I feel the sting of the braided leather against my skin. The first few strikes are painful, and I have to focus on relaxing and controlling my breathing. I crave this feeling—it silences my thoughts and allows me to be free.

Most people have the reaction Natalie did when she found out I was consenting to be whipped. They have visions of a bloody, battered body, but that's not what will happen—this is not abuse. Brandon and I negotiated every second of this scene. He's skilled with a whip and is able to bring me pleasure without bruising or cutting me.

My mind wanders, and I lose focus and start holding my breath. Without being fully relaxed, the impact of each lash is magnified. The scene is too intense. I brace for the next strike, but it doesn't come. Brandon is at my side checking on my color.

"What's your color, *mon petit papillon?*" he says, his breath cool against my sweat-drenched skin.

I stop and take a mental inventory before responding, "Green."

"You look so fucking gorgeous right now." Brandon rains kisses on my neck. "If we're going to keep going, you need to stop holding your breath. I want you to relax into each strike. Let everything else go. It's just you and me."

"Yes, Sir."

Why did I feel safe doing this scene with him? This right here. Brandon is so tuned into me that he sees those small changes, ones that will quickly put me at yellow, and knows to stop and check in. He breathes slowly and deeply with me until I'm back in a relaxed state of mind.

"I'm going to start again now."

"Thank you, Sir." I take a cleansing breath and ready myself to feel the whip make contact with my skin and penetrate deep inside. To the place where my darkest memories reside.

With each crack of the whip, the pressure gauge rises higher and higher until everything I've bottled up inside explodes. Tears stream down my face as I watch the memories, emotions, and nightmares rush away from me.

I'm free.

Light as a cloud drifting somewhere between wakefulness and sleep.

The scene is over. Although I can't talk, I can see, hear, and feel. The restraints around my ankles release. Brandon's speaking to me. He's telling me how proud he is of me. With each word, I soar higher. My wrists are released, and my arms fall limp by my sides. Strong arms lift me, and I rest my head on Brandon's chest as he holds me close, whispering words of devotion.

With the door to the suite closed, I can no longer hear the music from the club.

"I'm going to lie you down. I need you to roll onto your front," he instructs.

The bed dips as Brandon sits next to me. "This might sting a little." He squeezes Arnica gel from the tube and gently rubs it on my back. "Are your ankles or wrists sore?" I shake my head. "You did so well. I'm in awe of you, *papillon*." The breeze from the air conditioner vent overhead makes me shiver. "I'm going to cover you." Brandon pulls the lightweight blanket over me and lies beside me, holding me close.

Subspace is peaceful. There are no worries or pain, only softly spoken words of comfort and love. I want to stay here forever, but I have no control over what my mind chooses. Little by little, I become one with my physical body.

"Brandon," I whisper his name and reach for him.

"I'm right here." His arms tighten around me. "Welcome back. Do you need anything?"

"I'd love some cold water."

"I can do that." He smiles warmly. "I'll be right back."

I watch as he walks across the room to the mini fridge and marvel at how his muscles flex with every movement.

Brandon twists the cap off the plastic bottle. "Can you sit up?"

I push up onto my elbows and adjust to a sitting position. The cold water is refreshing on my dry throat.

"Take these." He passes me two acetaminophen from the little white bottle we left on the bedside table. "Are you ready to eat?"

"No, not yet." I screw the lid back onto the bottle. "I'm a bit sleepy."

Brandon climbs back into bed and lays down next to me. I rest my head on his chest, and he wraps his arm around me. "Sleep, *mon petit papillon.*"

"I don't want to miss the Shibari demonstration." A yawn escapes.

"There'll be others."

I don't have the energy to argue. My eyelids are heavy and close despite my futile protest. Sleep pulls me under its spell.

After a quick shower, I redress and meet Brandon back in the bedroom just as he's finishing cleaning up.

"Did we miss it?"

"I think so." My stomach growls loudly. "Hungry?" Brandon asks with a grin.

"Very."

"Come on. Let's go find Alex and Natalie and see if they want to get something to eat."

We emerge from the hallway and find the earlier crowd is beginning to disperse.

"Great scene tonight," Anthony approaches Brandon and gives him a congratulatory hug.

"Thank you. How did yours go?"

"It went very well." Anthony beams. He and his submissive, Leo, were scheduled to do a wax scene. I love watching them. Their chemistry is off the charts.

"Have you seen Alex?" Brandon asks.

"Yes, he and the girl are in the café."

I look in that direction and spot them. They appear engrossed in conversation.

Anthony glances over at them. "I haven't seen Alex that enamored by a woman in a very long time. Where's she from?"

"She's Lana's roommate."

"And she's a submissive?" he asks, surprised.

I can't help the laugh that escapes.

"No. My wayward sub is playing matchmaker tonight."

"I see." Anthony smiles. "It seems she's done an excellent job of it."

Brandon rolls his eyes. "Don't encourage her."

After saying our goodbyes, Brandon and I walk to the café.

I come up behind Natalie as she's saying, "I read all the books she gave me, but I still had a very different picture in my mind. Being here tonight, it's nothing at all like I imagined. Each couple we watched shared a genuine connection. There was nothing wrong about—"

"I'm so glad you liked it," I squeal and throw my arms around Natalie's neck.

I scare her, and she nearly jumps out of her seat.

"Great scene tonight." Alex stands and shakes Brandon's hand. "Grab some chairs and join us."

Brandon grabs chairs from an empty table and drags them over. "Are you enjoying your evening?" he asks Natalie.

"I've had a great time," she says, her eyes sparkling as she looks at Alex and then back to Brandon. "I think I'd like to learn more."

"The club has intro classes during the week. You should sign up," Brandon suggests.

When I got the idea of setting up my best friend with Brandon's best friend, I hoped they'd hit it off, but I never imagined it would actually happen. By the smiles on their faces, it looks like maybe they're headed in the right direction.

I hope it sticks. Alex and Natalie deserve to find happiness.

Brandon

WE SPEND THE NEXT FEW HOURS WITH ALEX AND Natalie in the club's café. The two of them can't keep their eyes off one another. I'll be the first to admit I thought Svetlana was off her rocker trying to set up her innocent roommate with my broody best friend. By some miracle, they hit it off. I haven't seen Alex this happy in years. If there's anyone who deserves a happily ever after, it's him.

"Oh, wow, it's almost two a.m. I promised Cinderella here I'd have her home early," Lana says and looks at me. "Sir, do I have permission to leave?"

"You did great tonight." I run my knuckles down her cheek. As much as I want to take her home and finish what we started earlier, that was never the plan. Svetlana wasn't sure how Natalie would react to everything she saw tonight. We agreed it was more important for Lana to be home with her to address any questions she may have. Fortunately, it seems she had a good time. "Go, get your friend home."

"Thank you for the tour, Alex."

He stands and kisses Natalie's cheek. "It was my pleasure."

I kiss Lana goodnight, and the girls head for the door. Alex remains standing, watching them walk away.

"Go after her," I encourage him.

"I don't know if I can," he says without taking his eyes off Natalie.

I nudge him forward. "You can't just let her walk away."

"Natalie," he finally calls and hurries to catch up with them.

I don't know what the future has in store for them, but if they can make each other happy, even for a short time, it's all worth it.

Svetlana

I'M IN MY ROOM PACKING MY BAG TO SPEND THE WEEK at Brandon's when Natalie appears in the doorway.

"Are you going to Alex's this week?" she asks, confused.

"No. I'm moving some of my stuff into Brandon's place."

"Moving in? You haven't been seeing him for that long," Natalie says, confused.

"Come in. We need to talk." Natalie sits on my bed, crisscross applesauce, she calls it. "Brandon and I have been together since right after I came to New York City."

"Why didn't you tell me?"

"At first, it was nothing serious." I try to explain. "Then, you were so freaked out by everything that happened that night. And all the BDSM stuff." I sigh loudly. "I was afraid of what you'd think, and I didn't want to lose your friendship."

I came to New York to escape being Maxim Solonik's daughter. It isn't that I'm not proud of Papa or that I'm ashamed of being his daughter. Actually, it's the opposite. I measure every man I meet by the example he's demonstrated with Mama. It can be suffocating, though. People judge me by how they judge him. Especially after Jelena was taken.

Despite being in the Bratva, Papa always kept a low profile.

The people in our community respected him. I was a happy little girl with friends—a normal life.

Until the day she disappeared.

Papa was ruthless in his search for her. He tortured and killed anyone who had anything to do with her disappearance. He never laid a finger on an innocent person, but that didn't matter. Our neighbors and friends no longer wanted anything to do with us. They were scared.

It wasn't until I went to university in Moscow and met Mei that I had another close friend, but time and distance have caused us to grow apart. I treasure my friendship with Natalie and don't want to do anything to destroy it.

"I was shocked that night, but I would never let something like that come between us. I couldn't imagine my life without you in it."

I swipe at the tear that escapes. "I treasure my friendship with you."

"Me too," she says sadly. "I wish you would've shared it with me. I could've supported you and been happy for you."

"I'm sorry. It doesn't feel like enough. I hope you can forgive me."

"I already do."

I've never met anyone like Natalie. I don't know how she forgives so easily, and I know I'm undeserving, but I'm incredibly grateful.

"So, you and Brandon are serious?" she asks.

"We've been all over the board." I chuckle. "But I think we've finally figured *us* out and signed a contract. I really like him a lot, Nat."

"So do I." She smiles. "I hope you'll give me the chance to get to know him better."

"I will. I promise."

Brandon: I'm outside. There's no parking, but if we switch off, I can come up and get your stuff.

Me: I only have one bag I can manage. I'll be out in a minute.

"Brandon's here." I zip up my bag. "Are you seeing Alex this week?"

"I don't think so. I have a big paper due."

"It's okay to put schoolwork aside and go out every now and then."

"I have to keep my grades up for the scholarship."

"Really, Nat? It's our last term before graduation, and you have a 4.0. I don't think you're in any danger."

"Have a good week." She hugs me.

"We're continuing this conversation when I get home."

Brandon carries my bag into his house. The door barely closes before he orders me to take my clothes off. I knew I'd be spending most of the week naked, so I didn't bring much with me. He dims the lights while I remove my pants and shirt.

"Where do you want me, Sir?

He smiles, and I see a mischievous glint in his eyes. "In front of the window."

"Yes, Sir." The curtains are partially open, allowing anyone outside to glimpse what we're about to do. When I get to the window, I turn around and watch as Brandon unbuttons his dark grey shirt. He slides it off his arms, exposing his toned body.

His chest rises and falls with each breath, enhancing the cords of sculpted muscles. My eyes lower to his abdomen, and the defined muscle that leads to a sculpted-V then disappears beneath the waistband of his pants.

I stare unashamedly as Brandon's hands move to his belt. His biceps flex as he opens the leather and works at his button and zipper. He lowers his pants and steps out of them. His cock is hard and tents the black boxer briefs that sit low on his hips.

"Do you see what you do to me, *mon petit papillon*?" Brandon's dominance takes up every inch of the room. I nod. "You're going to have to do better than that."

"I do." I manage to say. He hasn't touched me, and I can already feel my insides clench in anticipation.

Brandon closes the distance between us, and his mouth crashes against mine. My back presses against the cold glass, sending shivers down my spine. His hands tangle in my hair, pulling my head back as his mouth travels down my neck and lower. He draws my nipple into his mouth, sucking and nipping it. My hands roam his shoulders and back as I bask in the attention he gives first to one breast and then the other.

"Put your hands on the window," he orders. I watch over my shoulder as he lowers his boxers. He positions himself behind me and thrusts inside, pushing my breasts against the window.

A moan slips from my lips as he pulls out. His hands go to my ass, and I feel the tip of him press against me. My head drops back on his chest as he pushes past the tight ring of muscle. He takes me this way as often as possible, so my body accepts him readily.

His arm snakes around my waist, splaying his hand on my flat stomach, holding me tightly against him. "You're so fucking tight," he says and starts moving, rocking his hips into me. He slides his hand lower, leaving a trail of fire along my skin. His fingers dip inside my pussy, matching the thrusts of his cock.

"Do you like knowing someone can come by at any second and see me fucking you?"

"Yes." The word comes out breathy. The curtains provide a thin barrier between us and the outside world. My heart races with the knowledge that someone might walk by and see what we're doing at any moment, but I don't care. Nothing else matters except for the exquisite sensations coursing through my body. Brandon spears two fingers into my center. My body squeezes them as pleasure radiates in ripples.

His fingers pump in and out at a feverish pace. "I can't, please." The feelings are too big.

"You can." His fingers move to my overly sensitive clit,

rubbing circles. His cock grows impossibly hard inside me as he inches closer to his release. Brandon moves his free hand to my neck, putting the smallest amount of pressure against it. He thrusts harder and so incredibly deep. "Fucking come for me again, Svetlana."

An orgasm explodes, and my body shakes from the overwhelming crescendo. He thrusts one last time as his cock swells, spilling inside me. Brandon holds me against him, and our hearts beat in synchrony. I'm lost in the pure ecstasy of the moment.

When the last waves of pleasure have ceased, Brandon pulls out and steps back. Immediately, I miss the warmth of his body against mine.

"Let's go shower. I'm not through with you."

Svetlana

THE WEEK WENT BY FAR TOO QUICKLY. EVEN THOUGH it's Saturday, Brandon had to go into the office, and I have schoolwork I need to get done, so I had him drop me off early this morning. Natalie and I are sitting at the kitchen table having a cup of coffee while she tells me about her date.

"Last night was like a real-life fairy tale. Alex is amazing."

"I knew you two would get along." I just wish I had given her the benefit of the doubt and introduced them sooner.

"How long have you known Alex?"

"A little while."

"How long's a little while?"

This conversation cannot happen. Natalie may be able to handle the BDSM lifestyle, but I'm sure there's no way she'll be okay with Papa being in the Bratva. Thankfully, the doorbell rings. I don't know or care who it is. All that matters is it's a distraction. "I'll get it," I say, hurrying to the door.

"Saved by the bell," Natalie calls. "But this conversation isn't over."

"Alex," I say his name louder than necessary. "I didn't know you were coming over."

"Is Natalie here?"

"You bet. She's in the kitchen."

Natalie jumps up from her chair and tries to make a beeline for her room, but she's not fast enough.

"Good afternoon, Natalie." Alex's voice stops her in her tracks.

"Hi. Can you excuse me for a minute? I need to get changed."

"You look perfectly fine to me."

"I'm going to shower and study," I say in a sing-song voice. "I'll leave you two alone." As much as I'd love to stay and eavesdrop, it would infuriate Alex.

After a long hot shower, I blow dry my hair and throw on sweatpants and a T-shirt. The rest of my afternoon will be dedicated to preparing a closing argument for the mock criminal case my class is working on. I sit at my desk with my laptop and stare at the screen, but curiosity gets the best of me, and I crack the door to listen for voices. Natalie says goodbye to Alex, and the door closes.

"Is he gone?" I ask, peeking my head into the room.

"Yes, he just left. He had to work."

"And?" I walk into the living room and drop onto the sofa.

Natalie sits next to me and puts her head on my shoulder. "He brought a contract. Will you look it over with me?"

I want to squeal with excitement, but I school my features and keep my voice even. "I'd love to."

She grabs the papers from the kitchen table and returns to the sofa. I look through the four pages, making sure to read everything, which isn't difficult. It's a basic contract that reflects Natalie's newness to the lifestyle very well. It's reminiscent of the contract Slava offered me.

"What do you think?" she asks.

"I want to hear your thoughts first." I set the papers on my lap and look expectantly at Natalie.

"Alex and I went over each part, and I feel comfortable with it," she says hesitantly.

"But you're still worried about your scholarship and having to go back to Northmeadow."

"Alex said he was okay putting a time limit on it, but I don't think it'll be as cut and dry as he makes it seem."

Natalie was so desperate to go to NYU that she accepted a scholarship with a ridiculous work clause attached. At the time, she didn't think twice because she was planning to go back and marry Tommy. But everything's different now, and that scholarship is more like a ball and chain holding her hostage.

"Let me call Papa. He'll buy out your contract, so you don't have to go back."

"You're as bad as Alex." She blows out a frustrated breath.

"I'm just offering you a way out."

"And I appreciate it, but I can't accept it." She holds up the contract. "I want to sign this."

"Then, I think you should do it."

"I just don't know. It's not that simple."

"For once, don't overthink it. Just do it," I encourage her.

"I need to think about it. I don't want either of us to get hurt."

She hasn't said it yet, but I know she's going to do it. I'm happy for both of my friends. My only regret is that I didn't introduce them sooner, and because of that, their relationship will be short-lived.

Brandon

When Lana and I first got together, I had no idea what our future might look like. Little by little, it's become clearer. After graduation, she agreed to move in with me. Typically, I work long hours, and although Lana's studying for the bar exam, she insists on keeping the house and doing all the cooking. I've become very spoiled coming home to a hot meal and a woman I love every night. Our lives have become very domestic, but that hasn't damped the flames of our relationship.

The past few months have been trying. Alex was in Russia working closely with Maxim and Nicholai Federov, one of Maxim's close associates. I worked even more than usual, keeping the company going with the actual marketing accounts and everything on the trafficking network end.

On top of work, Lana and I were helping Alex with his plan to propose to Natalie—which he did yesterday, Christmas Eve. I'm not entirely sure how he pulled it off, but he planned an entire day of surprises before the proposal in Central Park. It was no surprise that she said yes.

"Wake up," Lana says. "It's Christmas."

I don't bother opening my eyes. "The sun isn't even up yet."

"But other things are." She moves down my body and takes my hard length into her mouth. My eyes roll back in my head.

Lana's mouth feels exquisite. I let her control the pace as she gently runs her teeth along my dick before paying extra attention to the sensitive tip. She runs her tongue along my slit, blowing gently before slowly taking me into her mouth.

It's my turn to take over. I wrap her hair around my hand and lift my hips. Lana relaxes and lets me use her mouth. Over and over, I push her head to the root of my cock. She takes everything I give until I shoot ribbons of cum down her throat. I let her hair go, and she licks me clean.

"Merry Christmas, Sir," she says as she sits back on her knees.

After I give her pussy the same attention with my mouth, we shower and go downstairs to exchange presents. It's the perfect Christmas morning. Outside, the ground is already covered in white, while more fluffy snowflakes float on the cold breeze. We're in the middle of opening our gifts when my cell rings.

"Merry Christmas and congratulations," I answer the phone.

"Brand." Alex's voice is strained.

"Is everything okay?"

"No. We're on our way to Northmeadow. Natalie's father was shot."

"Shot?" I ask, certain I misheard.

I put the phone on speaker as Alex tells us that Natalie got a phone call around four a.m. informing her that her father had been shot in a robbery gone wrong. Tommy, her ex-boyfriend, broke into her family's pharmacy, looking for drugs. Stanley had recently installed a silent alarm system, and rather than calling the police, he decided to go to the store himself. During the confrontation, Tommy shot him.

"How bad is it?"

"He was shot in the chest and life-flighted to Branson for emergency surgery," Alex explains. "All the office could tell us is that things don't look good."

"Can I talk to Natalie?" Lana asks through her own tears.

"She's not up to talking right now."

"Tell her I love her, and we'll be praying for her father."

"Keep us updated when you can."

"I will. I have to go. We're pulling into the airport now."

Lana walks over to the window. "This isn't fair." Her body shakes from the force of her crying.

I wrap my arms around her, and she rests her head on my chest. "Life rarely is."

"This was supposed to be one of the happiest days of their life. Now, it'll forever be mixed with tragedy."

Stanley sustained a direct hit to his right lung. He was in surgery for nearly twelve hours to repair the damage. Even then, the odds weren't in his favor. It was a huge relief to everyone when Natalie texted Lana yesterday to tell her that her dad was awake and breathing on his own. There's still a lot of uncertainty, but things aren't as bleak as yesterday.

While Lana's out for a run with Pyotr, I check my work email. While I'm scrolling through my inbox, Alex calls.

"Hello?"

"I fucked up. Natalie safeworded." His voice cracks. "She left me."

I was expecting an update on Stanley, so it takes a beat for me to process what Alex just said. "What happened?"

"I bought out her contract and handed her resignation to the school district."

"Shit, Alex. I thought we talked about giving Natalie the freedom to make her own choices?"

From day one of their relationship, Alex begged Natalie to let him buy out her contract. As much as she dreaded having to return to Northmeadow, it was important to Natalie that she fulfill the promise she made.

He and I have had this conversation a million times, and each time, we come to the same conclusion. Natalie needed to be able to handle this on her terms.

"That was before her psycho ex almost killed her father." His voice cracks. "What do I do now? I can't go after her. My hands are tied."

"You really dug yourself a hole this time."

"I was terrified and reacted. I realize it was too far now, but I don't know how to fix it. I need to get her back. I don't want a life without Natalie in it."

"Where are you?"

"I'm in Branson. I can't leave."

"Let me talk to Lana, and I'll call you back. We'll figure this out."

After we hang up, I drop my head into my hands. The gravity of the situation weighs heavily on me. But as much as Alex wants me to swoop in and fix this, I don't know that it's my place to intervene. While I understand exactly why Alex did what he did, he also overstepped a boundary.

"Natalie just called," Svetlana says, bursting into my office. "She safe—"

"I know."

"You do?" she asks, surprised.

"Alex called."

"What are we going to do?" She sits in the chair across from my desk.

"Nothing."

"What do you mean nothing?" she asks, her voice growing louder. "We can't just sit by and watch this happen."

"Yes. We can." I try to sound more confident than I'm feeling. "I can't believe this. I'm going to shower." Lana storms out of the office.

The reality is that I have no idea what I'm supposed to do. They're our friends, but should we insert ourselves into a situation that doesn't involve us?

After going back and forth, I decide we need to stay out of it. Alex and Natalie need to work this out for themselves.

They'll get through this—I hope.

Svetlana

"Please don't keep shutting me out," I say on Natalie's voicemail for what has to be the hundredth time. "I'm here when you're ready to talk."

It's been nearly three weeks, and Natalie still won't take my calls.

"No luck?" Brandon asks when he walks into the kitchen.

"I left her another voicemail. Did you get Alex?"

"Yes. He's still in Branson." Brandon sits across from me at the table.

"I know you said we need to stay out of this, but—"

"I booked us a flight into Northmeadow tomorrow," Brandon says, and my jaw drops. "Natalie will be driving back to Northmeadow tomorrow to pick up some things for her mom. She'll be spending the night."

"Really?"

"Yes, really."

"How do you know this?" I ask.

"I know people in high places," he says, laughing at his joke. "Alex bought a cottage at that lake outside of Northmeadow. He had it renovated. It was supposed to be Natalie's Christmas present, but they never got that far."

"Why didn't you tell me?"

"Alex asked me not to." I grin. "He's on his way there today. Our job is to get Natalie to the cottage."

"And how do you propose we do that?"

"We have until tomorrow evening to figure that out."

Our plane landed at the small airport in Northmeadow in the late afternoon. We had enough time to rent a car and drive to Clarke's house, where we've been parked, waiting for Natalie to show up. It's been close to two hours, and the sun is just beginning to set.

"Are you sure she's coming?" I ask impatiently.

"I'm sure."

How do you— Never mind, there she is now." I spot the beat-up silver car she lovingly nicknamed Rhonda, the Honda. She pulls into the driveway and shuts the engine off but makes no move to get out. "Do you think she saw us?"

"I don't know," Brandon says as he watches in the rearview mirror. "There's no reason to wait here. Let's do this."

The words are barely out of his mouth when I open my door and jump out, running toward her car. I know the second she sees me because she throws her door open. She's barely to her feet when I wrap my arms around her.

"What are you guys doing here?" she asks, looking between me and Brandon, who's standing off to the side.

"We're here for an intervention. Can we come in?"

"An intervention?" Natalie asks hesitantly.

Brandon walks over and gives her a hug. "All we ask is that you hear us out. If it doesn't change your mind, we won't say another word about it."

"Okay." I can tell from the tone of her voice that she's not sold on the idea.

"I have to get the groceries." She opens the trunk and grabs a few bags. Brandon gets the rest, and we follow her into the house.

"Just put them on the table." Natalie puts them away quickly. "Can I get you guys something to drink?"

"Water would be great," Brandon says.

"Make yourself at home." Natalie motions to the sofa in the living room.

The mood is tense while I help her get the drinks. She doesn't say anything to me, which makes this even more awkward. With our ice waters in hand, we join Brandon. I sit next to him, and Natalie sits across from us in the old, worn chair that's her father's favorite.

That's when I get a good look at her. She's exhausted. Her eyes are puffy, and she has dark circles under them from not sleeping. On the ride here, Brandon told me that Viktor's been keeping an eye on Natalie from a distance. She's been driving back and forth trying to manage her parents' pharmacy and everything at the hospital. If something doesn't give, she's going to end up in the hospital, too.

"Alex is miserable. And you aren't much better," I blurt.

"It's been a rough few weeks. But it'll get better, eventually."

I've rehearsed this part in my head since Brandon told me the plan yesterday. Now's the time, but I'm terrified. I look at Brandon, who gives me an encouraging smile. I haven't even started speaking, and I'm already getting emotional. I swallow over the lump in my throat and start.

"I need to tell you a story. It's not something I like talking about, but you need to hear it." Natalie doesn't respond, but she watches me intently. "I'm not sure where to start. So, I guess I just say it. My papa is a *pakhan*, the boss of a group in the Bratva."

"You expect me to believe Maxim's in the Russian mafia?" she laughs.

"Yes." My answer is matter-of-fact.

"And I thought there wasn't anything more you could tell me

about Maxim that'd surprise me. But what does that have to do with Alex?"

"I had a sister," I say, fighting back tears. "Jelena was five years older than me. She was smart and beautiful. I wanted to be just like her. I was ten years old when she was taken. We were walking down the street when two men jumped out of a van and grabbed her—we were holding hands, and they ripped her away. Jelena yelled at me to run and not look back." I swipe at the tears that are now falling.

"I had no idea. I'm so sorry."

"They were traffickers. Papa searched day and night, but even with all his connections, it was too late when he found her. She'd already been sold and killed. Since then, Papa's used his position in the Bratva to fight the traffickers. He couldn't save Jelena, but he has saved many others."

Silent tears slip down Natalie's cheeks as she listens to the secret I've kept for so many years.

"It's made him very overprotective of me. So, when I approached Papa and told him I wanted to come to America to study, he went crazy." I laugh. "He wouldn't be able to protect me here, which was unacceptable to him."

"I'm sure he was terrified something would happen to you. But I still don't see what this has to do—"

I put my finger up, stopping her. "Hang on. I'm getting to the part about Alex." She takes a sip of her water. "Papa didn't want to hold me back, so he arranged for me to stay with a business associate of his who lived in New York. This is where Alex comes in." I smile. "My parents and Alex's parents had been friends for many years. Which is how Papa started working with him in the first place."

That got Natalie's attention. She adjusts her position on the chair.

"Papa's responsible for reintroducing Alex to the lifestyle. He knew that after Alex's Mom passed away, he lost his focus—his direction. The first anniversary of his mom's passing was a particularly bad time for Alex. Papa found him drunk in his room. He was concerned about him and stayed with Alex the rest of the night. The following morning, he told Alex about his friendship with his parents and invited Alex to the club. Initially, Alex was resistant. He wasn't interested in having a sub. But my papa can be persuasive, and Alex finally gave in."

"That's how Alex got involved at Fire and Ice."

"It is. Fast forward a few years. The businessman Papa went to visit was Alex. Papa asked if he would step in and become my Dominant."

"You and Alex were a couple?"

"Alex and me?" I raise my eyebrows. "He's a great guy, but he's not my type. We were never a couple."

"What Lana's trying to explain." Brandon steps in to help. "Is that Maxim asked Alex if he'd be willing to be responsible for Lana's safety. To allow her to wear his collar of protection."

"Doesn't wearing a collar symbolize a relationship—ownership?" she asks, clearly confused.

"In some cases, yes, but there're other kinds of collars," Brandon explains. "Lana was young and would be alone in a big city—in a foreign country. She was also a submissive who would be playing at a new club. Maxim wanted to ensure Lana had someone willing to protect her in his absence. A protection collar doesn't represent a partnership but rather a Dominant's commitment to be responsible for another's safety. It also meant any Dominants interested in Lana couldn't approach her without getting Alex's permission."

"So, you and Alex were never together?" Natalie asks.

"Nope, never a couple. Never played together." I reach into my purse and pull out the collar with the locket. I hold it out to Natalie. At first, she doesn't move, but finally, she takes it and examines it closely. "That was my collar. On the charm, you can see Alex's initials and the lowercase p to show I was under his protection."

Recognition sweeps over her face. "You wore this when I first met you."

"I wore it for almost six months." The memories are bitter-sweet. "I was so lonely until Alex showed me the city and introduced me to his friends at the club. Without him, I probably would have packed up and gone back to Russia. But it wasn't always smooth sailing. Alex can be a bit overprotective. He made decisions for me that I didn't always agree with."

Brandon laughs a full belly laugh. "Alex and Svetlana became famous at the club for their very heated disagreements. Star and Owen had to step in on more than one occasion." Natalie cracks a small smile.

"The thing is, he saw things and knew things I didn't. It was hard, but I had to learn to trust his decisions. And in the end, he was always right."

She passes the collar back, and I drop it into my purse. "This isn't the same, Lana."

"It is, Nat. You may not see the big picture. Actually, I know you don't see it."

"When Alex lost his mother, he gave up. He closed himself off from everyone around him. He was afraid of caring about someone and losing them, too. Then you came into his life, and his carefully constructed walls crumbled," Brandon says. "All those fears rushed to the surface when your dad was shot. When you told him what Tommy did to you that night, it pushed him over the edge. I'll admit, he made some rash decisions."

"That's an understatement," she adds sarcastically. "Alex and I had an agreement, and he broke it."

"I agree with you, Natalie. Alex and I have discussed what happened. He knows he was wrong and understands that he should've approached things differently. Alex is a Dominant, a protector—sometimes to a fault." Brandon pauses. "He's also only human, and sometimes he screws up. But Alex is a good man. All he was thinking was that he couldn't risk losing you. I know you disagree—"

"Disagree? I more than disagree."

"That man loves you." Brandon's expression changes, and the Dominant emerges. "Do you love him?"

"Yes," she says softly.

"Do you trust him?"

"Brandon—"

"This lifestyle revolves around trust. Do you trust Alex as your future husband and, more importantly, as your Dominant?"

Natalie looks down at her hands, fidgeting with her fingers for several long seconds. Finally, she looks back up. "Yes, I trust him."

"Get your coats, girls," Brandon says. "We're going for a ride."

I jump up and grab my coat, but Natalie doesn't move.

"Where are we going?"

"This time, you have to trust me." Brandon has a playful grin on his face. "Get up. Let's go."

I grab Natalie's hand, and she reluctantly follows me.

When we're all seated in the car, Brandon turns around. "One more thing. You need to put this on." He holds out a blindfold.

"You're seriously crazy. You know that?"

She swipes the fabric from his hand and puts it over her eyes.

"Good girl. Sit back and relax."

Brandon looks at me, and we share a knowing smile. I can only imagine what Natalie's thinking as we drive to the lake. Finally, we're making the final turn onto a gravel road that leads to the cottage. Brandon puts the car in park and says, "You may remove the blindfold now."

Natalie slides it off, her eyes blinking a few times while they come into focus. She looks out the window at the enchanting stone cottage set amongst the trees. Luminaires line each side of a path leading to the front door.

"It's gorgeous. But what are we doing here?"

"Go knock on the door," Brandon says.

"But I don't—"

"Stop questioning, and just trust me." Brandon corrects her. "Get out and go knock on the door."

Natalie exits the car and takes a few tentative steps before looking back.

"Keep walking," Brandon encourages her through the open car window.

Reluctantly, she continues walking. Before she gets all the way to the door, it swings open. A nervous-looking Alex stands in the doorway. He says something to Natalie before giving us a small wave. That's our cue to leave.

"Do you think they'll be okay?" I ask.

"I do," Brandon reassures me.

Brandon

ALEX AND I HAVE BEEN IN ALMOST CONSTANT CONTACT the past week. There's been a series of security threats on the encrypted files we hold for Maxim. Viktor's checked them out and assures us they're coming from inside the office. That sets my mind at ease somewhat. Since Alex is still in Missouri, it's up to me to find out what's going on.

My office phone rings.

"Hello?"

"Mr. Carpenter," Paul, our front desk attendant, says. "Ms. Solonik is here to see you."

"Please send her back."

Lana's only come to the office a few times and never unscheduled.

"I hope I didn't interrupt anything," Lana says as she appears in the doorway of my office.

"Nothing that can't wait. Is everything alright?"

"I wanted to discuss this guy I'm seeing." She closes and locks the door. "He's been spending more and more time at his office. I'm afraid he's having an affair with his receptionist."

"Given the fact that his receptionist is a man," I say and walk around my desk, closing the distance between us. "And he's only interested in women. One woman in particular. I don't think you have anything to worry about."

"I thought it was important I come to check things out for myself. You know, stake my claim and all." She smiles.

"And how do you propose to do that?"

Her hands go to my belt, opening it, and then move to my pants and boxers, sliding them down my legs as she lowers to her knees. I'm already hard with the anticipation of what she's about to do.

She drags her tongue from the base of my cock to the top and looks up at me for a second before opening her mouth and taking me in. I close my eyes, savoring the feel of her warm mouth wrapped around me.

Lana alternates between gently sucking and lightly dragging her teeth up my cock. Releasing it from her mouth, she uses her hand, pumping up and down before taking a finger and sliding it through the pre-cum that's gathering at the tip.

She looks up and gives me a wicked grin before taking me in until I hit the back of her throat. At the same time, she uses her lubricated finger to slide into my ass, earning a deep throaty groan. She massages the area gently at first while licking and sucking my cock. She adds more pressure with her finger as she takes me in her mouth deeper and faster.

I grab her hair and wrap it around my fist, needing to control the pace as my orgasm builds from deep inside. Her finger massages inside me harder and faster. "Fuck, Lana," I growl as my body convulses inside her mouth. Wave after wave of cum shoots down her throat. Lana doesn't stop massaging me as she swallows everything I give her. A moan escapes my lips, and my legs nearly give out from the force of the orgasm.

Finally, my body begins to come down from the high. Slowly, she pulls her finger out and circles the tip of my dick with her tongue before releasing me.

Without a word, she pulls my boxers and pants back up and closes them. I grab her neck and pull her to me, kissing her deeply.

"Will you be home on time tonight?" she asks, still breathless.

"I'm afraid not," I say, releasing her.

"Are you going to tell me what's going on yet?"

"Not here. I'll talk to you at home tonight." The office's walls tend to have ears, and I don't want anyone overhearing the information I've learned.

She kisses me. "I'll have dinner waiting."

"I'll text you when I'm leaving the office." Lana turns to leave, but I grab her waist, stopping her. "Be ready for reciprocation when I get home."

It's killing me to watch Lana walk out the door, especially after that, but Alex is flying in tomorrow, and I have information to put together that he'll find very interesting.

Alex and I met late last night to form a plan for today. When I looked into what was happening in the office, I found two employees venturing out on their own, a move Alex always supports—except this time. Rather than doing things in an honorable way, these two are trying to poach Alex's personal clients. They might've gotten away with it, except they tried to access Alex's encrypted files. I'm certain they thought they would access information about some secret clients. Unfortunately for them, they set off alarm bells that are about to expose their plan.

I meet Alex in the conference room after the last of the employees have filed in. Our security guards are coming this way. They'll be waiting outside until they're needed. I give them a nod before closing the door and joining Alex at the front of the room.

"If everyone can take their seats. I want to keep this short so we can start our weekend early," Alex says, waiting for everyone to turn their attention to him. "First, I'd like to congratulate Cameron and Morgan on signing two new clients to the agency this week." Applause and congratulations fill the room. When they die down, he continues, "I want to thank Brandon for steering the ship while I was out of town. Everyone's done a great job keeping the day-to-day operations running seamlessly. I appreciate you all. I'll open the floor for any questions."

Several employees ask questions about some outstanding accounts. Alex and I address them quickly. "Anyone else?" No other hands go up. "I have one more thing, and then you can go. It's come to my attention that several of your colleagues are branching out from Montgomery Advertising to start their own company. Ben and Michelle, please make your way up here."

Alex and I step aside, allowing Ben and Michelle to bask in their short-lived success. The unsuspecting pair smile proudly, believing their secrets are safe. They're about to experience Alex's ruthlessness, something few ever experience.

"These two employees came to my company fresh out of college. Over the years, they've worked hard and achieved a remarkable amount of success." he pauses, giving them several more seconds of false security. "Typically, I support employees taking the next step and opening their own company. But that isn't going to happen." Their smiles disappear as they look at one another with confused expressions. "Ben and Michelle made the mistake of trying to steal my clients. Your personal belongings are waiting at reception. Security will escort you out of the building." Alex opens the door, and our security team steps in.

The room is shrouded in uncomfortable silence as Ben and Michelle take their walk of shame.

"Now that that's out of the way," I address the remaining employees. "Does anyone have anything to add before we wrap up?" When the shock of what just happened begins to wane, heads shake, indicating no questions. "In that case, have a great weekend."

Everyone grabs their things and says goodbye on the way out.

"That went well," I say.

Alex drops into a chair. The stress of the afternoon weighs heavily on him. "I'm just glad it's over."

I know Alex is in a hurry to get back to Natalie. "Lana's out with the girls tonight. I'll drive you to the airport."

With that pressure off at work, I'm free to put more time and attention back where it belongs—on Svetlana and me.

Svetlana

BRANDON AND I FLEW INTO BRANSON LAST NIGHT. Today, we're driving to Alex and Natalie's lake cottage. We'll be joining Anthony and Leo, Alex's dad and his sub, Luna, and Natalie's parents to celebrate the July Fourth holiday. There's very likely to be more fireworks than what's in the sky when Natalie's parents meet Anthony and Leo.

I haven't seen Natalie in seven months, which makes the hour-long ride feel like it'll never end.

"You're driving me nuts," Brandon says. "Stop tapping your fingers on the door."

"I didn't even realize I was doing it."

"We'll be there in a few minutes."

"I don't know if I can wait that long."

Brandon laughs. "You don't have a choice."

He turns the car onto the bumpy gravel road that leads to their cottage. It looks much different during the day. Brandon parks off to the side, and we get out of the car. We're getting our bags from the trunk when the sound of tires crunching the gravel draws our attention. Natalie's parents are right behind us.

"Go on ahead," Brandon says. "I'll get these."

"Are you sure?"

"Yes. Once Charlotte gets in there, neither of you will get a word in edgewise."

"Thank you." I plant a kiss on his cheek and hurry into the house. The front door is open, so I walk in. I spot Tony and Leo in the kitchen. "Something smells good in here."

"Hey, girl," Leo says.

"Do you know where Natalie is?"

"She's in her room getting dressed."

"Thanks." I hurry down the hall and stop at the only closed door. "You going to be in there all day?"

The door swings open. "I can't believe you're here!" Natalie squeals and throws her arms around my neck.

"I wouldn't miss this for anything in the world." I squeeze her back. "Your parents were just pulling up when we walked into the house."

"Lana, I'm so nervous. What if they hate everyone?"

"Not even Charlotte could hate Leo."

We both laugh.

"I hope you're right." She grabs my hand. "Come on, let's go say hi."

Brandon

TODAY HAS TURNED OUT TO BE A RELAXING DAY. ALEX and Natalie were worried about everyone getting along, but everything's gone smoothly. Dinner was a huge success, something that doesn't come as a surprise to me. Tony's cooking is incredible. Now, everyone's gathered around the fire pit, enjoying a spectacular sunset that'll eventually give way to tonight's fireworks display over the lake.

I have a surprise of my own for Svetlana. I've been waiting for the perfect time which I've decided will be tonight during the fireworks.

While we're talking and enjoying one another's company, a tense-looking Viktor appears in the doorway and motions for Alex to go inside.

"I wonder what's going on," Lana whispers.

"I have no idea. I'm sure it's nothing, though."

A short time later, Alex emerges from the house just as the fireworks light up the night sky. He takes his seat and pulls Natalie onto his lap. I'm about to make my move when Lana's phone chimes. She pulls it out and opens the text message. I read it over her shoulder.

PapaL There has been a development with the computer

attacks at Alex's office. You and Brandon are to stay at the lake tonight. Tomorrow, you will all leave for JFK. My jet will meet you there. We will be staying at the compound until further notice.

Lana: I understand.

She schools her features and slides the phone back into her pocket. Lana and Alex exchange a tense glance before she settles against my chest and returns to watching the fireworks.

I'm not sure what's going on, but whatever it is, it must be important if Maxim's calling everyone to the compound. My plans for tonight are going to have to wait.

Stanley and Charlotte leave right after the fireworks conclude. We're all still gathered at the firepit when Alex and Natalie return from saying their goodbyes.

"Are you going to tell me what's going on now?" Natalie says, her hands on her hips.

"No. Sit down," Alex says quietly. "We have guests."

Natalie ignores him. "I saw the look between you and Lana earlier. What's going on?"

The mood shifts from relaxed to awkward.

"I think it's time we turn in," Anthony says with an exaggerated yawn.

"You don't have to. Don't let my wayward sub chase you away." Alex narrows his eyes at Natalie, issuing a silent warning.

"It's really okay," he says and motions to Leo, who's kneeling at his feet. "It's time for us to turn in anyway."

Lana pulls Natalie aside and whispers something. Hopefully, she's trying to talk some sense into her. Natalie doesn't break her stare down with Alex as she shrugs.

I decide it's time we make an exit and let Alex deal with this privately. "Lana, we should go too."

"No, you two need to stay."

"Oh?" I ask, hoping Alex gives us a hint as to what's going on.

"Dad, I need you to stay too."

"Luna, go to bed. I'll be in shortly," Sam Montgomery says to his submissive.

"Let's move this inside," Alex says. "I'll get Viktor and meet you in the living room."

It's only a few minutes before Alex and Viktor enter the room.

"There was another attempt at accessing the encrypted files earlier today." He takes a deep breath. "I was wrong from the beginning. The files weren't being accessed from within the company."

Lana takes my hand in hers, the only outward sign of her nerves.

"It wasn't the employees you fired?" Sam asks.

"No. The timing of everything was purely coincidental."

"Is Max aware?"

"Yes. He called earlier. His jet's enroute to JFK. We're leaving in the morning for an extended stay in Russia."

"We're what?" Natalie spins around. "We can't do that. My parents. Our bridal shower." Tears pour down her face.

Alex hurries to her and takes her by the shoulders. "We don't have a choice."

"I'm not going to Russia."

"Come with me." Alex struggles with keeping his temper under control. He takes Natalie by the arm and walks her outside.

"I'll get your things and move them into my cottage tonight," Viktor suggests. "I think these two are going to need some time alone."

While Alex was finalizing the purchase of their cottage, the one next door also became available. He bought it so Viktor could set up their security and have a private place to stay.

"That's a good idea. Do you want a hand?"

"No, I've got it." Viktor disappears down the hall to get our things.

Sam, Lana, and I exit through the front door and walk to the other cottage.

"I thought everything was taken care of," Lana says.

"So did I. This is a total shock."

"My heart aches for Natalie," Sam adds. "She's not handling this well."

"She's dealt with a lot the past few months," I say.

"I don't think she understood the full extent of what Alex's involvement with Max entailed."

Viktor catches up with us.

"Is Nat okay?" Lana asks him.

"I don't know. I didn't see them." Viktor sets us up in one of the guest rooms. "If you need anything, let me know." He leaves, closing the door behind him.

I sit on the bed and drop my head into my hands.

"What's wrong?" Lana asks, sitting next to me.

"Everything."

"It's not that bad. The compound's incredible. You'll love it there."

"That's not it." I sit up and turn to face her. "This is not how tonight was supposed to go."

"What are you talking about."

I reach into my pocket and pull out the small box I've been carrying all day. "I had everything planned. It was going to be perfect." I open the box, and Lana gasps.

Inside is a three-carat princess-cut diamond set on a platinum band with flowing ribbons of beaded milgrain and diamonds.

"Brandon," she says, bringing her hands to her mouth.

"Every time I go to do this, something else comes up. I'm done waiting for the perfect time." I drop to one knee. "The first time I met you, when you walked into Alex's kitchen, time stood still. You took my breath away. Since then, we've had our fair share of hurdles. Through every trial fate through our way, our connection was an unbreakable thread weaving our destiny together." I take one of her shaking hands into mine.

"I'm sure our trials aren't over, but I know that as long as we face them together, we're invincible." I wipe a tear from her face. "You're the sun that brings light to my darkest days and the compass that guides me through life's stormy seas. You breathed life back into me. Svetlana, I love you with all that I am. I can't imagine my life without you by my side. Will you do me the honor of becoming my wife?"

Silence hangs between us as I wait for her answer. "Yes," she whispers the one word, the only word I hoped she'd say.

I slide the ring onto her finger before standing. Leaning over, my lips meet hers as I push her softly onto her back. My hands go to the hem of her shirt and begin sliding it over her body when there's a knock on the door.

"Who is it?"

"It's me," Viktor says.

I get to my feet and open the door. "What's up?"

"I'm sorry to interrupt, but there are a few things we need to go over."

I look over my shoulder at Lana, who's sitting up, examining the ring.

"Give me a minute."

"No problem."

I close the door and walk back to the bed just as Lana slides the ring off.

"What's wrong? Don't you like it?" My stomach sinks.

"I love it."

"Then why did you take it off?"

"Our engagement should be a time of great joy. Whatever's going on is very serious, or Papa wouldn't make us all go to the compound. I don't want to start our forever with a dark cloud hanging over us." She places the ring in my palm and closes my fingers around it. "Will you ask me again when this is over, and we can celebrate?"

"You deserve no less than perfect, *mon petit papillon*. As soon as this storm passes, I'm putting this ring back where it belongs."

"There's nothing I want more."

I pull her to me and kiss her deeply. "I have to go see what Viktor needs. I expect you to be on your knees waiting for me when I return."

"Yes, Sir."

Our engagement is important enough to wait until nothing else overshadows it. I leave the room, both disappointed that she's not wearing a token of our promise and overjoyed with the knowledge that she's mine.

Maxim's men are highly skilled. We'll go to the safety of the compound while they figure out where the threat is coming from and eliminate it. The second they do, Lana and I will be free to share our good news.

Our happily ever after is just around the corner.

When Lana runs from Brandon to escape her pain, she discovers that the truth cannot be outrun. In the final chapter of their story, they face the ultimate test of love, forgiveness, and healing. Start reading *Mended Hearts* today and experience the powerful conclusion to their unforgettable journey.

Also by Tara Conrad

Find Tara's Books Here

About Tara

Tara Conrad is the author behind sizzling and passionate love stories that ignite the senses. Her novels celebrate the fiery intensity of desire. They are known for having a blend of deep emotional connections, relatable characters, and captivating plots that ensnare readers from the very first page to the last.

Tara's the mother of four incredible, kind, and talented adult children. She also has one son-in-love who will always be her favorite. She's also Nana to the more perfect little boy- E.J. He's the little owner of her heart.

Tara is married to her soulmate and Dominant, George. They recently celebrated their 30th anniversary and are more in love today than yesterday. George encouraged Tara to start writing, and with each passing day, she's more thankful for his insistence that she tell her stories and his partnership on this journey. There is no one else in this world she'd ever want by her side. He is her happily ever after.